And she saw him, a single man sitting by the window.

Not her type, with his whipcord-lean body, that taut intensity, but she found herself unbuttoning her sweater, tossing her hair out of her eyes.

As if he felt her attention, he turned and looked at her straight on, and Miranda felt a kick in her chest. His eyes were incredible—the thick lashes lent a deceptive innocence, but there was nothing of the child in the direct way he seemed to look right past all her barriers.

He stood up and gave her a slight inclination of his head, a courtly gesture, and extended his hand.

"Hello," he said. "You *must* be Miranda."

Dear Reader,

Colorado is a place where people take their exercise outside—hiking and biking, running and skiing, walking and strolling and gardening. And there's a good reason for it. Even indoor girls like to be outside on a day as brilliant as the one outside my window right now—mild temperatures, sunny skies, the mountains standing up in crystal-clear clarity on the horizon. Every weekend from March to November you'll find me on the trails, hiking with my friends.

But Colorado is also land of the extreme athlete—a marathon to the top of Pikes Peak and back? A 100-mile run at altitudes above 10,000 feet? (100 miles??) I can't imagine doing such feats, but I love the idea of people who have the will. I fell in love with one—a runner who ran to the top of Pikes Peak in his fortieth year, and his passion for running is where this book came from, though, of course, fiction takes on a life of its own.

Miranda is a city girl who finds herself falling under the spell of James Marquez, the sexy long-distance runner of rare integrity who shows up in Mariposa. See how it all works out for them—and for Miranda's sisters, Juliet and Desi Rousseau.

Warmly,

Ruth Wind

RUTH WIND

Miranda's Revenge

Silhouette®

Romantic

SUSPENSE

SILHOUETTE BOOKS

ISBN-13: 978-0-373-27549-6
ISBN-10:   0-373-27549-8

MIRANDA'S REVENGE

This edition published by arrangement with Harlequin Books S.A.

Visit Silhouette Books at www.eHarlequin.com

Printed in U.S.A.

Books by Ruth Wind

RUTH WIND

A passionate hiker and traveler, Ruth Wind likes nothing better than setting off at dawn for a trip—anywhere! Her favorite places so far include the Tasman Sea off the coast of New Zealand, the aromatic and pungent streets of New York City and the top of her beloved Pikes Peak. Between books, she's currently planning trips to India, China and a long rest in the damp and misty United Kingdom. Explore her columns on rambling around France and Scotland, working the marathon to the top of Pikes Peak and many topics about the writing life at www.awriterafoot.com.

Ruth Wind also writes women's fiction under the name Barbara Samuel. You can visit her Web site at www.barbarasamuel.com.

With love to Christopher Robin.

Chapter 1

A light snow started to fall as James Marquez made his way from his hotel to a coffee shop. It was May, and technically too late, but so high in the mountains, snow could fall at any moment and often did. He tucked his hands into the pockets of his old jean jacket and lifted his face to the sky. He'd grown up in New Mexico, where the sun seemed to shine relentlessly, endlessly, and he loved inclement weather.

This was very wet snow, fat raindrops that had crystallized at the very last second and lost their shape immediately upon landing. Big flakes caught momentarily in the cup of a red tulip growing in a pot by the door of a shop. The sight—white snow against the satin red petal, yellow stamen poking out—made him pause.

As if to emphasize the whimsy of the combination, sunlight suddenly broke through the dark but scattered clouds and painted a rainbow into life.

He paused, grinning. An old man stopped and looked at him. James lifted his chin toward the vivid display. "God's showing off."

The man, a little stooped and skinny, his skin weathered to freckles, glanced over his shoulder and nodded. "He shows off a lot around here." He paused, big hands hanging at his side, and admired the arching rainbow for a moment, then eyed James sharply. "You in town for the run?"

"Partly."

"I ran it every year myself till three years ago. My wife made me quit." He rubbed his nose, grown too long for his lean face, and scowled. "Don't know what difference it makes if I die of a heart attack in the shower or while I'm running."

"You can take the runner out of the race," James said with a grin, "but you can't take the runner out of the man. What was your best time?"

"Three forty-three back in 1967," he said. "I was forty-nine years old."

James whistled, long and low, and stuck his hand out. "I won't even get close, but let me see if some of that power'll rub off on me."

The old man smiled, shook his hand. "I'll be cheering you on."

The sun had come out, and James lifted a hand in farewell. The old man headed in his own direction.

Less than four hours. Good grief! Speaking of showing off. The Mariposa 50K Trail Run was one of the toughest in the country, up and down steep mountain passes and through forests and over the top of rocky ridges, on very uncertain footing at times. To have made such a time forty years ago was pretty amazing.

With sudden awakening, James realized who the old man had to be—Peter Bok. "Holy cow," he muttered aloud, and turned around, but the man was gone.

Peter Bok. It seemed a very sweet sort of blessing. James grinned and saluted the sky. "Thanks, man."

Miranda Rousseau felt vaguely exhausted as she walked down Black Diamond Boulevard in Mariposa, Colorado. A faint headache knocked at the back of her skull, something that seemed to happen whenever she had to think about her mother. Not an hour ago, Carol Rousseau, brilliant scientist and narcissistic social butterfly, had called to airily announce she would be arriving in Mariposa in three days so that Miranda's father could run some stupid race on Sunday.

Three days. Which would put them in town for more than a solid *week* before Juliet's wedding. Miranda didn't think she could stand to be in the same town with her parents for two *days,* much less a week—and yet, there was not a single freaking thing she could do about it. They were coming. Miranda's sister Juliet was getting married. They'd all have to just pretend to be one big happy family for a little while.

As if they could.

Miranda took a long breath of mountain air, trying to shake the phone call from her shoulders. It would be such a waste to think about her parents when she was in the middle of one of the most beautiful places on the planet. Resolutely, she focused on the scene around her.

A few minutes ago, when she'd set out, snow had been falling. Now, sun spilled from between the clouds, a gold that seemed to splash across the streets, dance on the clattering leaves of cottonwoods that lined the river, puddle in corners and curl up with pots of geraniums blooming in front of the shops decked out for summer tourists, who would arrive to hike and fish and visit the expensive spa tucked up in the forest.

Not many tourists had yet arrived, though she'd seen a handful of backpackers, mostly students who took refuge in the hostel. The ski slopes had been closed for three weeks, but the snow up higher was not yet completely gone. It would be another few weeks, the first of June, before the summer crowds would arrive.

Which only meant that Miranda would likely be able to find a table by the window at the ReNew Café, an all-organic café and gift shop she loved better than any other place in Mariposa. The staff played world music and wore hemp clothing, and some of them had dreds, eccentrics who made her feel comforted so far from her East Village digs. She was only here for a month, to help plan the last of the details for Juliet's wedding—D-Day was May 25—and recharge her batteries. And maybe see if the three sisters could keep one of them out of jail.

Which was why Miranda had come to ReNew this morning. She had arranged to meet with a private investigator, who was the only one of many she'd called who was willing to drive as far as Mariposa. It had been a highly publicized case, splashing the newspapers a couple of months ago, and most of the investigators had felt there was nothing to be discovered. It appeared to be a clear cut love triangle that had ended with a wife killing her adulterous husband. Clear, simple, banal.

However, Desi was innocent, and unfortunately would go to jail for killing her husband if they could not find the real killer.

Miranda suspected most of the investigators didn't want to make the long drive into Mariposa—seven hours over looping mountain roads from Denver. The man who'd agreed to meet her was coming from Albuquerque, a little less grueling drive, but he had an ulterior motive. He was one of those crazy runners who participated in the Trifecta of Trails, a series of three extreme runs in the Colorado Rockies, one of which would take place in Mariposa on Sunday—a 50K run at more than ten thousand feet.

The idea made her head ache. Who'd be crazy enough to run thirty-one miles at high altitudes, climbing and descending sometimes one thousand meters? Lunatics. Only lunatics.

And—she blinked in recognition—her father. Why in the world was he doing such a thing? He wasn't a runner of *that* caliber! And it wasn't like he was young. He'd kill himself.

Anyway, the P.I. from Albuquerque wanted to run the Mariposa, and that was fine with Miranda. If he could find out who really killed Claude Tsosie, Desi wouldn't go to prison for it. Which it seemed more and more likely she would if somebody didn't do *something*.

Magenta geraniums in clay pots bloomed on either side of the door to ReNew, and a giant Siamese cat sat in the retail side of the window near Miranda's own St. Chocolata, one of the tongue-in-cheek *nichos* she'd managed to mass-market to great popularity. Seeing it temporarily eased her slight headache. Life wasn't so bad if she could make a nice living as an artist. How many people could say that? It was a great blessing, and she needed to focus on that. How blessed she was, not how cursed.

Humid air washed over her, redolent of cinnamon and coffee and spices mingling with hints of exotic incense. Miranda breathed it in, feeling tension ease from her neck. A gentle reggae tune played on the speakers, and the boy behind the counter gave her a nod as she put her sunglasses on her head, looking around the room.

It was quiet enough now, with little knots of locals, mostly young, scattered around the tables. A girl with a tangled ponytail and a backpack typed at a bank of computers against the wall. On the retail side of the house, where racks of T-shirts and tourist take-homes and bumper stickers lined the room, a pair of women in their forties chuckled over a bank of cards printed on recycled paper. She wanted to stand there and see if they'd go over to her St. Chocolata—and forced herself to look away. And saw him, a single man sitting by the window.

Zounds, she thought, surprising herself. Not her type, with his whipcord-lean body, that taut intensity, but she found herself unbuttoning her sweater, tossing her hair out of her eyes.

He sat in a pool of sunlight, like a cat. The light glanced off a thick pelt of dark hair, beautifully cut to fall across his brow, not too long. Cheekbones like mesas, a perfect Johnny Depp mouth, a jaw like the edge of a table, so clean and straight and hard. His eyes were large and dark.

Miranda tended to go for big, hearty blondes, but there was definitely something going on with her spine, which was buzzing like a fluorescent light, and her hands felt too big, the palms tickling, itching, the way they did sometimes when she wanted to paint. There was, in the harsh angles and softness and colors of his face, a beauty that kindled something to life in her artist's heart. He would make a beautiful saint, a prophet, with those sharp, clear lines.

As if he felt her attention, he turned and looked at her, straight on, and Miranda felt a kick to her chest. His eyes were incredible—the thick lashes lent a deceptive innocence, but there was nothing of a child in the direct way he seemed to look right past all of her barriers, right to the center of her, like a priest or a sage might do. He didn't seem to care that he was staring, that she had halted right in the middle of the restaurant, and couldn't seem to go forward.

He stood up and gave her a slight inclination of his head, a courtly gesture, and extended his hand. "Hello," he said, "You *must* be Miranda. Not many people can have hair like yours."

She'd told him she had long red hair. "Probably not," she said, gathering a hank of it in her hands, and in nervousness, spread some of it over her palm, examining the red-gold waves. "I know it's sort of stupidly long, but I can't seem to ever do more than trim it. It's like a limb."

"Nothing to apologize for." His voice was low and calm, Steadying. He gestured toward the spot opposite him at the table. "What would you like?"

Miranda fluttered to the chair and perched on the edge of it, tossing her hair over her shoulder to glance at the menu, which was chalked on a board over the counter in neon colors. Sunflower Muffins was scribed in green and yellow; Blueberry Scones in purple and white. "What are you having?"

"Coffee," he said, still standing. Waiting.

"Oh, please," Miranda said, "sit down. I'll get it in a minute. When I decide."

It could not be said to be a smile, but something lightened in his face. "Please, allow me."

Miranda shook her head, stood up. He was a little taller than her own five-ten, but not much. Still she liked having to lift her chin a little to look up at him. "I called you. The treat is mine."

"Trust me, you'll pay plenty for my services, Ms. Rousseau." He gestured her back to her seat, inclined his head. "Chai? And…I think a cinnamon twist."

It was her order every day. "How did you know?"

"A trick of my trade," he said with a quick wink.

Flustered, she tried to think what gave her away. Maybe she didn't look like a coffee drinker. Maybe the paisley print of her peasant blouse made him think of India, thus the chai. But how would he figure out the cinnamon twist? There were dozens of choices in the glass cabinet.

Seeming to sense her confusion, the man took pity and smiled. "The boy at the counter told me. You're a regular."

"Oh." Miranda blinked. Gathered her scattered brain. "You must think I'm an idiot. I've just got this silly headache this morning, and—" She broke off. "Never mind. Chai and cinnamon twist is fine."

He moved away silently, as graceful as an antelope. Miranda turned her head away stubbornly and stared out the window. Water dripped down from the roof and tip-tapped to the sidewalk below. A pair of female athletes in wicking T-shirts and running pants strode by on sturdy thighs, the hair on their arms glinting in the sunlight. Miranda watched them with her hand on her chin. What would it be like to be an athlete? To spend your days in physical pursuits and feel all that muscle all over you?

The investigator sat down across from her. "I did not introduce myself," he said, and now she heard again the soft, musical lilt of someone who spoke Spanish, perhaps not as a primary language, but certainly on an equal footing with English. "I am James Marquez."

She accepted his handshake. A cool, strong hand, she noted. Confident grip, but not overbearing. None of that funny business men sometimes indulged, either, sliding his palm along hers, holding it too long. "I appreciate you coming so far," she said.

"No problem."

"You have the race anyway, right?"

He lifted a shoulder. "I'm intrigued by this case, honestly, but the race didn't hurt." He grinned, leaning forward with boyish excitement. "Do you know who I just met? Peter Bok."

Miranda blinked. "Obviously I should know who that is, but I'm afraid I do not."

"A famous runner. He took the Mariposa 50K seventeen years in a row, and set a record that still hasn't been broken."

"Wow. He lives here?"

"He's old now. Really old, but it's cool, anyway."

Cool, Miranda noted. Who said cool these days? She nodded. Coolly.

As if he felt her disapproval, he tugged a little notebook out of the inside pocket of his jean jacket and flipped it open. "Let's get started then. You want to find out who killed your sister's husband, right?"

"I don't know everything," Miranda said. "We'll have to talk to my sister to fill in all the details—she's currently out on bail. But basically, the police don't have much except strong circumstantial evidence that all points to my sister Desi."

"What kind of circumstantial evidence?"

"She had some of his blood on her clothes, and they'd had a fight the day before, right outside here, I think," she said, pointing to the sidewalk just beyond the windows. "About half the town heard her threaten to kill him."

"Because?"

"Because he'd taken a mistress."

He nodded. "And she had opportunity?"

"Unfortunately, yes. She was tracking a mountain lion who'd killed some goats. Or maybe sheep. Something." She waved a hand. "Anyway, a rancher had shot the lion, but didn't kill it, and Desi went out to track it."

James raised his head. His pencil was still between his long, dark fingers. "She threatened to kill him," he repeated. "She had his blood on her clothes, *and* she was tracking mountain lion with a rifle when he died?"

Miranda lifted a shoulder. "It sounds bad, I know."

He simply looked at her. "How do you know she didn't do it?"

"I don't," she replied. "Not in any provable way. But I do know, the way you just know somebody. Desi might have been furious with him. She might have done all kinds of things to make him mad, but she wouldn't *kill* him."

"People do all kinds of things in the heat of passion."

"Yes." She looked out the window. A patch of purest blue showed between a frame of clouds, and she shook her head. "I don't know how I know she didn't do it, but I *am* absolutely sure. And anyway, it doesn't matter, does it? You don't have to decide if she did or not—you just find the true killer."

"What if it turns out to be your sister?"

Miranda took a breath. "I guess we cross that bridge when we come to it."

He measured her without speaking, his eyes still and calm, his face expressionless. Miranda, known for unflappability, met that gaze with her own, letting him see that she meant it.

But it wasn't easy to keep herself from looking away. His irises held the liquid depth of fondue, and somehow, she kept wanting to look at his mouth. He was impeccably shaved.

"All right," he said finally. "When is your sister scheduled to go to trial?"

"June 4. We managed to get it pushed back so Desi could at least be in our sister Juliet's wedding." One of the benefits of a small town, Miranda supposed.

James tapped his pen on the page, pursing that fabulous mouth. "I'll do what I can between now and then to see if we can find another killer. You'll be billed my daily rate, as well as incidentals, and I require a deposit of two days up-front." A soft-sided briefcase was propped next to his chair and he bent down to draw out a sheaf of papers. "Here is a contract. Take it with you and look it over, and you can let me know what you decide."

Miranda took it, a single page setting out his rates

and what was included in the fees and what he billed as an extra. "Looks pretty straightforward," she said.

"Oh, yes, a small addendum to this one." He held out his hand and Miranda gave it back to him. He hand-wrote an addition, and gave it back.

Miranda grinned. "Prerace, race and recovery day are not to be billed. Very good."

He blinked and she had a sense that she'd startled him somehow. "Do I know you from somewhere?"

She shook her head. Smiled slightly. "No. I'm sure I'd remember." He frowned and she added, "Unless you follow the art world. I'm an artist. I've been in some magazines and the Sunday style sections in a few places."

"Not really." He continued to look at her steadily, sorting through the possibilities. "But you do look very familiar. Very."

She twisted her mouth. "Or maybe you saw me in the tabloids. I was mixed up with an Olympic skier for a while last spring."

"Not likely."

Miranda shook her head. "I don't know then." The Siamese cat ambled over and rubbed against her leg, purring loudly. Miranda leaned over to scratch his back—and then it dawned on her. She smiled at James. "I bet I know. Come with me."

Without waiting to see if he followed, she lifted the cat with a grunt and headed into the retail area of the café. "Did you look around in here?"

James came behind her, dressed in jeans and a soft,

long-sleeved shirt that wasn't quite chambray. Maybe polished cotton? The blue kindled a warm hue in his tanned skin. "Yes."

She pointed to a photo of herself propped on an easel nearby a display of her altars. "That picture?"

He grinned and came forward. "Good detective work."

"Thanks." She held the cat close, his tail swishing elegantly over her arm, his body a vibrating pulse of purr.

James paused and surveyed the altars. St. Chocolata of the Cookie Jar, St. Renegada of the Dance Floor, who wore blue sparkles and high heeled shoes. "These are yours?"

"Yes."

He bent closer.

"I hope you're not one of those Catholics who don't have a sense of humor," Miranda said.

He straightened. "Not at all. Are you?"

Miranda smiled. "Touché."

"I should be going," he said. "I have an appointment with a mountain this afternoon. Will you call me when you know what you want to do?"

"I already know we want to hire you. I can pay you now."

He looked at his watch. "Would it be possible for you to meet me at my hotel at about five? We'll go over details then, and I'd like to talk with your sister Juliet and, was it your brother-in-law?"

"Yes. Soon-to-be brother-in-law. He's a tribal police officer on the Mariposa Ute Reservation, right outside of town. Juliet—not Desi, who is the one in trouble—is marrying Josh in two weeks." She thought of her parents again for the first time and sighed.

"You don't want them to get married?"

"What? Oh, no—I was sighing over something else. My parents are coming to town in a couple of days." She raised an eyebrow. "My father thinks he's going to run the Mariposa 50K."

"Your father is a runner?"

"He's lots of things, but yes, runner is one of them."

"And you don't have a good relationship?"

Miranda rolled her eyes. "No. My parents are—" she paused for effect, looked at the horizon, back at him with a bright smile "—narcissistic vampires."

He raised his chin, smiling just enough to make his eyes crinkle at the corners. "I see."

"You don't," she said with resignation. "No one does."

James laughed. The sound of it was as rich as cup of cocoa. Everything about him was chocolate, she thought whimsically. Dark chocolate hair, milk chocolate eyes, Viennese chocolate flesh. "You'd be surprised."

The cat wiggled in her arms and Miranda let him go. "I'll see you at five at the Hotel Mariposa, then."

James took her hand and met her eyes directly. "I am looking forward to it."

She told herself the tingle in her wrist and shoulder was just a pinched nerve. Behind her, St. Chocolata chuckled.

When James wandered out, Miranda turned to the

little statue. "Oh, shut up," she said, and headed back out in the day to tell her sisters the good news.

And the bad news, she thought, remembering her parents.

An extra week! Ugh!

Chapter 2

James spent the warmest part of the day running the toughest stretch of the race course, six miles of switchbacks and steep inclines on scree-covered trail, in the full brunt of sunlight. High altitude sunlight was a killer, he knew from his own childhood, and since Colorado—like his native New Mexico—was generally sunny, chances were good he'd face this hard sunlight on race day.

It was demanding, but he was pleased at his performance, and made some notes to himself about how to add to his nutrition slate. He ran back to the hotel and showered, ate lunch and headed over to the police station to see what sort of reception he could scare up.

At the Mariposa station, he was met with the chilly stonewalling he'd expected, though they did tell him to come back and talk to Sergeant Moore if he wanted. He wanted. They wouldn't make him an appointment, but begrudgingly admitted the Sarge had headed to the closest "big" town—Gunnison—and would be back at suppertime.

His next stop was the library to read on the Internet everything related to the case. He Googled the main players: Desdemona Rousseau, a veterinarian with a large animal practice in town and a wolf rescue center on her land in the mountains; her late, murdered husband Claude Tsosie, a Native American artist; Christie Lundgren, an Olympic skier and Claude's mistress; and a tangle of businessmen, politicians and land developers. He made notes and created a list of questions.

After he made his notes there, he headed over to the local newspaper offices, the *Mariposa Times,* which had covered the story of Desi and Claude from the beginning. Taking out the reading glasses he cursed every minute of every day, he perched them on his nose and scrolled through hundreds of inches of copy on the murder and the ensuing investigation.

Glamorous life he led.

By the time he returned to the hotel for his late-afternoon meeting with Miranda, he had amassed a number of facts and a long list of questions. It was a lot more complicated than he'd originally imagined. Maybe Desi *was* innocent, despite the fact that ninety-nine percent of the time, a spouse was the culprit when an unfaithful partner was found dead. But he had a nose for things, and in this case, a lot of people would have gained something from Claude Tsosie's murder.

The Hotel Mariposa took up an entire block. Built in 1875, at the height of the Colorado gold rush, it was suitably ornate, appointed with carved wood and elegant banisters and enormous blocks of stained glass depicting stories from classical mythology—Diana and her wolves, Persephone and her descent into the underworld, and a copy of Botticelli's Venus, rising from an oyster shell.

The vast center lobby rose seven stories, the room opening onto balconies that circled upward and upward to a conservatory roof made of wrought iron and glass netted with chicken wire. He wondered how it survived the hailstorms around here. Obviously it did.

On the ground floor, trees—some probably at least fifty years old—grew in gigantic pots, and an eye-popping display of bougainvillea splashed downward from each level, the fuchsia-colored blossoms glowing in the cool light.

It was a great spot. James was glad one of his buddies—a skier who loved the Mariposa slopes—had tipped him off to it. His room was a little on the small side, but it looked both into the atrium and to the San Juan mountains, and boasted a claw-foot tub he'd love after punishing his body in the race.

The lobby was busy, with ectomorphic runners of both sexes and many ages checking in and sipping lemon water at the huge, heavy bar. He wasn't the only one here early to put in a few hours in training. The race was in three days. He would rest on Thursday and Saturday, very easy runs. Most of them would.

Amid the runners, a handful of family groups, honeymooning couples and vacationers were mixed in, along with the usual hard-drinking college kids.

Miranda stood out as vividly as if a spotlight shone down from the ceiling. Perched on the edge of a tapestried chair in a simple white blouse and a fluttery green skirt, she looked like a Botticelli, with her rippling red hair and long limbs and the wide, smooth oval of her face, dominated by eyes the color of the Albuquerque mountains, deep, deep blue.

She didn't see him immediately, and he was pleased to have a moment to compose himself. She was exactly the sort of woman he tried to avoid—beautiful, troubled, fierce, independent. She didn't need a man, didn't want one, and yet, passion leaked like a damp fragrance from every pore on her body.

Which he wouldn't mind licking, head to toe.

The thought, bawdy and vivid, shocked him. He was not the kind of man who ordinarily had such thoughts, and yet, there it was, along with the others he'd been hearing since first setting eyes upon her in the coffee shop.

Lots of thoughts. Hot and elaborately detailed erotic thoughts.

He paused and took a breath, let it go slowly. Ridiculous. All his life, he'd seen what heedlessness did to a person, to families, to lives. He wouldn't indulge the fantasies, and eventually, they would go away. When he'd composed himself, he moved forward. "Hello, Miranda. I hope you haven't been waiting long."

As if startled, she turned abruptly, but didn't stand. "Hi. I saved you a spot. I was afraid it might get busy in here."

Her blouse gaped just enough that, from this vantage point above her, he could see nearly all of her right breast, a supple expanse of flesh ending in a bra made of cream lace. His forehead burned and he had to swallow hard to move his gaze away.

With his head down, he said, "Thank you." He settled on the chair next to her. Their knees pointed diagonally toward each other. A lock of her hair fell on the arm of the chair. Brilliant, glistening, shiny as metal.

To give himself a moment, he flipped open his notebook. "I came up with a few questions."

"Wow," she said, leaning forward to touch his notebook. "Isn't that a Clairefontaine?"

He raised his eyebrows. "Yeah. My sister sends them to me. She lives in Paris."

She said reverently, stroking the surface, "The paper is so smooth. I love it."

"Yeah," he said, and cleared his throat. "But you tell anybody I said that, and all deals are off."

She grinned. "I suppose liking French paper might undermine a man's image a bit."

"You think?" He flipped to the page where he'd written his questions in blue ink, and took out a black pen now. "I spent the afternoon getting up-to-speed, and I've got a lot of questions here."

"Okay. Let's get to those in a minute. I have some things for you first." She handed him a manila envelope. "The signed contract and a check for your first payment."

He accepted it, tucked it into the soft-sided case he carried. "Thank you."

A woman dressed in black jeans and a golf shirt with the name of the hotel on the breast stopped, a tray in her hand. "Can I get you two something? Fat Tire is on special today."

"Fat Tire?" Miranda echoed.

"Ale. Made in Colorado."

"I'll have one," she said. "James?"

He shook his head. "I'm in training. Just water, thanks."

"Ah," Miranda said as the server scurried away. "A true runner. My father never gives up his martinis."

"He doesn't run to win."

She blinked and then a tiny smile moved over her pink mouth. "You speak your mind."

"More than I should, probably."

She measured him. "Do you run to win?"

What he thought was, *why run any other way?* What he said was, "I try."

"Do you have a chance?"

"To take my age group, yes."

Her eyebrows raised. "I'll be at the finish line to see what happens, then."

He grunted.

"Or will that make you nervous?"

"No," he said. "There are a lot of people on the finish line, usually. One more won't make a difference."

"I see." A cool wind blew through the words.

James cleared his throat quietly. "That sounded rude. I apologize. It's just that, after that far, you're not really thinking about anything except how much it hurts."

"Ah." With a quizzical frown, she asked, "Why do it if it hurts?"

"To see if I can." Even talking about it, he felt the lure of the upcoming run in his limbs, tugging at his calves and ankles, his lungs. It was never possible to explain to a nonrunner why the pain after ten miles or twenty—or in this case, twenty-one—felt so exhilarating. He'd stopped trying.

She leaned forward and he saw another flash of her cream-encased breast. A buzz moved along the outside of his ears. "If I were to make a *nicho* to the saint of running," she asked, her long white hands laced together lightly, her forearms resting on her thighs, "what would she be called?"

"Anything you want. There is no patron saint of running."

"There must be. There's a saint for everything."

He lifted a shoulder. "There's not."

She inclined her head. "That's very interesting. I'll have to see what I come up with."

"Irreverent."

She met his gaze, her mountain-blue eyes snapping.

"Yes." She added no apology and he liked her for it. He smiled, and for a moment, he let himself look at her, and she looked back, and something unwound from his chest, his shoulders.

The server brought the drinks, and James took advantage of the moment to flip his notebook to the relevant page. "Can I ask my questions now?"

Sitting in the hotel lobby, with the murmuring sounds of other conversations filling the space of the atrium like swishing water, Miranda felt abuzz. Her limbs were fizzy. The back of her neck prickled. She wanted to stare and stare at James Marquez with his chocolate hair and chocolate eyes and burnished cinnamon skin.

But she forced herself to be professional. "I'll answer what I can, but we might want to talk to my sisters and soon-to-be brother-in-law. They're going to meet us in a half hour, if that's convenient for you." She plucked a single peanut out of the bowl on the table. "I wasn't actually here when it all happened."

"That's fine. Are they coming here?"

"No, Desi's partner runs a pub just down the street, The Black Crown. You'll like him—he's a New Zealander, an ex-rugby player, and the pub is wonderful—he has beer from all over the world, if that's your thing."

He gestured at the glass of Fat Tire in front of her. "It must be your thing."

"I spent a semester in Oxford and adore English ales, I have to admit."

Was it her imagination or did a shutter fall between them? "I'll keep that in mind."

"Oh, right. You don't drink while you're in training," she said, and found herself fluttering a hand toward his knee, away. "Would you rather meet somewhere else? It's just a good place to get some supper, too, and I know you need plenty of carbs if you're running like that. He has plenty of that kind of stuff, too."

"We can meet there, that's fine."

She inclined her head slightly. "So why am I getting the feeling that you've gone all stiff on me?"

It was only as the edges of his lips came up the tiniest bit that she realized the double entendre. She grinned. "Or actually, chilly, is what I meant, but I think I've teased you into a grin, haven't I?"

A sideways smile made his eyes crinkle at the corners. "Hard to resist."

Miranda let go of a bark of laughter, nudged his knee with her fingers. "So, tell the truth, Monsieur Marquez. Do you disapprove of drinking?"

He shook his head. "I don't drink much except beer—just never developed a taste for it, but I can't say that I'm terribly sophisticated about it." He picked up his water, sipped it, scanned the bar. "I haven't had much chance to travel."

Ah, a proud man. "I was born with terrible wanderlust," she admitted truthfully. "I can't remember a time when I wasn't dreaming of far away." With a shrug, she added, "When you want something that much, you tend to make it happen, don't you think?"

"How old were you?"

"Nineteen," she said, smiling. "Perfect timing. I was dying to escape my parents, and they paid for my semester, then I spent the following summer backpacking with some other kids all over Europe."

He nodded, still a little stiff, and Miranda wanted him back, focused on her, that thrumming, shimmering thing going on between them. "So where were you at nineteen?"

"Seminary."

Miranda let go of another burst of laughter, thinking of her irreverent saints. "Oh, brilliant!" She shook her hair out of her eyes. "Did you become a priest?"

"I did."

Her heart fell. "Are you a priest *now?*"

"No."

"Oh, good." She put her hand on her chest. Then she realized she'd tipped her hand, and bowed her head. Embarrassed.

"Are you blushing, Ms. Rousseau?"

"I could be, *Monsieur.*"

"That would be *Señor,* wouldn't it?"

She laughed. "I suppose it would." Then she sobered and looked at him, curiosity welling up like a monster. "I would like to hear your story," she said frankly.

"Not likely," he returned with as much directness. "I don't tell it very often," he said, his hands laced between his legs, his large eyes direct. Maybe too direct. She found herself sliding toward the fall, the dive into those dark, deep irises, wanting to put her fin-

gertips on the edges of his eyelid, brush the thickness
of his lashes.

"I suppose not."

Then that direct gaze shifted, swept over her face,
touching her hairline and brow, her lips and throat, her
chest and hands. Miranda raised her eyes and smiled,
very, very slightly. The silvery connection blazed for a
moment, as they exchanged visions of what might be to
come, what they might whisper to each other in a future
moment, when there was no murmuring of other voices,
no barriers of clothing, nothing but their bodies and skin
and voices, trading secrets. A distinct prickle burned over
her flesh at the thought, rolling from throat to groin, nape
to hips in a sudden wash that made her touch her brow,
lift the big glass of ale and take a long, cooling swallow.

"Maybe," he said in a gruff voice, "we should go
over a few things here."

"Sure. Absolutely." She took a breath. "What do
you need to know?"

"Let me look at my notes," he said, and flipped
through the pages of his notebook.

As she waited, the movement of a man caught the
corner of her eye. She couldn't say what it was, what
familiarity in the shift of a shoulder, the gesture of a
hand, but she raised her head just as he turned around.
A solid Austrian type, blond, tanned, very handsome
and leanly muscular. A skier.

Next to him was a blond woman, beautiful if her lips
had not been pursed in such peevish annoyance. Also
a skier, and one Miranda knew. "Uh-oh," Miranda said.

James raised his head.

"This is not good," she said, and found herself perching forward on the seat of the chair, ready for flight.

The couple had not seen them yet, but it was only a matter of seconds. Miranda grew aware of a wash of nerves burning through her, but was it over him, or her? Impossible to tell.

And what was he doing here, anyway?

"Isn't that Christie Lundgren?" James asked.

"Yes," Miranda said. "The skier."

"The woman Claude Tsosie was having an affair with, am I right?"

"Yes." Miranda's gaze was fixed on the pair.

"And who is that with her?"

"Max Boudrain." Miranda's voice was flat. Max shifted, putting his hand on Christie's elbow, tossing a heavy duffel bag over that powerful shoulder. He scanned the room, arrogantly, noticing everyone and no one.

Except Miranda. His step faltered, noticeably.

She stood with as much grace as possible under the circumstances. "Hello, Max. What brings you to Mariposa?"

"Miranda," he said in his nearly perfect English. "How wonderful to see you."

She felt snared by his very, very blue eyes, fixed with that intensity he had upon her face, and he came forward, limping slightly. She only realized as he bent toward her that he was going to kiss her cheeks, in Continental fashion, and there was no time to pull away. His hands—those hands that had explored every inch of her skin, had uncovered secrets she'd never known about her body—captured her upper arms, and then his lips brushed one cheek, then the other.

Backing away slightly, she stammered, "What… why are you…shouldn't you be in Peru or somewhere training?"

He gestured toward his leg. "A minor accident. I am not to ski for another month." He gestured toward the woman, her tousled blond curls artlessly sexy. "I am staying with my friend Christie. Are you acquainted?"

Friend. Did that mean girlfriend or not? Probably not. Max wasn't the type to be coy. "No," Miranda said politely. "Of course I know your reputation, but I haven't had the pleasure of meeting you." She extended her hand. "Miranda Rousseau."

Christie stiffened, and Miranda realized too late that she should not have mentioned her last name. Desi had not taken her late husband's name when they married; she, too, was a Rousseau. "I don't think I should be talking to you," she said, pulling back. "Nice try."

"*Excuse* me?"

"You won't get any information from me, or from Max, so forget it."

"I had no intention of—"

"Miranda and I are old friends," Max said smoothly. He gave a nod toward James, who'd come to his feet in polite fashion when the couple had approached. "Max Boudrain," he said, holding out his hand.

"James Marquez. I watched you in the Olympics. Two golds, right?"

He shifted his head. "Yes. And you, are you here to run the Trifecta?"

"Among other things, yes. I am."

Max smiled stiffly. "I see."

Christie glowered. "I'm leaving." She stormed away, all sleek cat fitness and blond good health.

Looking after her with an expression of bewilderment, Max said, "I'm sorry. She is not ordinarily rude."

Miranda waved a hand. "She has good reason. Her ex-boyfriend—" She broke off, waved a hand. "Oh, never mind. Let her tell you."

"It was good to see you," Max said. He nodded at James. "Perhaps we'll have a drink while I'm here, yeah?"

"Sure," Miranda said, though she had no intention of going. "Call my sister Juliet. She's in the book."

He nodded, his mouth still and sober. Miranda wanted to turn away, but he caught her hand, pressed his thumb to her palm. "It is very good to see you, Miranda."

She pasted a false smile on her face, gently pulled out of his grasp. "You, too, Max," she lied.

Chapter 3

James watched the exchange between Miranda and the skier with the practiced eye of a trained priest. Miranda's body was slightly angled away, her head often dipped left, her chin arrowing over the skier's shoulder, her gaze indirect.

Boudrain, in contrast, reached for her unconsciously, his hand lifting, then falling, his body tilting down toward her. James could see they'd been very passionate lovers. A beautiful couple, he judged, ignoring the flicker of possessiveness that made him wish to push between them, seize Miranda, fling her behind him.

The vision startled him. Ridiculous. She *was* beautiful. Healthy. His body responded to the moist allure of her, and his mind threw up pictures in response. Just like, he told himself, the times his body needed particular vitamins and his brain gave him pictures of oranges or pinto beans.

Forcing his attention away from Miranda, he took a moment to study Christie up close. She had been the murdered Claude Tsosie's mistress when he died. The notes showed a rock-solid alibi; at the time of Tsosie's death, Lundgren was drinking in the company of a dozen others, three of whom had seen her home.

As with Max, he knew her face from watching the Olympics on television. Both had won gold medals, and both had been media darlings, in part for their beauty, but also because of their talent. Max had taken a gold and a silver, in slalom and giant slalom; Christie had taken the gold in women's downhill, a long and difficult challenge.

In person, she was smaller and more delicately made than she seemed on television, bundled in ski clothes. Also, there was a vulnerability about her heavily lashed blue eyes that made her seem like a fierce but frightened animal. Her thighs were the strong, powerful legs of a skier, but her face was finely boned, her chest small.

He didn't think she and Max were lovers—they used the body language of siblings, none of the leaning in and pulling toward that lovers would show. Her expression when she looked at Miranda was not jealous, but sharp and angry. "Come on," she said to Max. "We can't talk to her!"

She practically tugged him out, as if Max was attached to Miranda by some invisible cord.

When they left, Miranda picked up her barely touched glass of ale and took a long swallow, then dropped a couple of bills on the table. "We should head over to the pub," she said. Soft color burned beneath her pale cheeks.

"Old lover, I gather?"

The color deepened. "Yes. Was it that obvious?"

"Not a good ending?"

She tossed her hair over her shoulders. "He's a professional athlete. Not technically, of course, but sports will be his life."

"And?"

"And men who are in the spotlight are too much trouble. Musicians, sports stars, actors, writers, painters, even professors—if they're in the public eye, women put themselves in their paths, and even with the best intentions, they'll usually be unfaithful eventually."

"That's a harsh assessment. Did someone break your heart?"

She narrowed her eyes. "You are direct, aren't you?"

"Saves time." They headed into the evening. Cool air, tinged with glacial edges, swept off the mountains rising in spectacular display around them.

"Max broke my heart," she said tightly, and put on her sunglasses, even though they were not strictly needed.

He smiled. "Take off your glasses, Jackie. The view

is great and I won't ask any more questions. At least about your personal life."

"Jackie?"

"Yeah, as in Onassis? Known for her glasses?"

"Oh. Of course."

He smiled down at her, feeling a tenderness all out of proportion to the moment and their acquaintance. She took off her glasses, stuck them back in a case in her purse, not on top of her head. Her vibrant blue gaze lifted to his.

"Now I can see your eyes," he said, and switched gears, trying to keep his focus on the business he was here to tackle. "So, Christie was Claude's girlfriend, right?"

"Yes."

"And by all accounts, she adored him."

"He was a very good-looking man, charming, artistic." She raised an eyebrow cynically as if to say, *see?*

"I saw the photos," he said, and scowled, nagged again by something odd. "What nation is he? I thought it was Navajo."

"Maybe. Desi will know. Does it matter?"

"Not really. Just—" he stepped to one side to let a woman and her dog pass on the narrow sidewalk, smiling when she dipped her silver head at him "—maybe it's the photos I saw, but he doesn't look Indian at all to me."

Miranda inclined her head. "Really."

"I'm no expert, of course, and genetics are weird, but I grew up around a lot of Indians and he sure doesn't look Navajo. Or Apache. Tsosie is a Navajo name."

"What benefit would there be in pretending to be Indian, though?"

"There must be some."

Miranda nodded. "I guess. Some artists joke around about becoming authentically ethnic in some way, to bring more value to the work. New York and L.A. both go crazy for authentically not-white."

"I can see that."

They crossed a narrow street, and passed through long bars of sunlight, arrowing between buildings. Miranda's hair caught fire, sparkling with gold and red and a dozen other colors. Of course she did not notice, only walked along with her astounding cloak shining like something from a vision. James forced himself to stop staring.

"Here it is," she said, pausing before a door propped open to allow an exchange of air. Cheerful voices spilled into the street.

James waved her ahead, and followed her in. The smell of frying onions made his stomach growl. She paused momentarily just inside the door, and he took a moment to look around while his eyes adjusted. The room was decorated in the fashion of an old English pub, with heavy beams in the ceiling and wide, weathered boards on the floor. Rugby jerseys lined the walls, a sport about which he knew little. He knew enough to recognize the jersey of the New Zealand All-Blacks, a team that carried a mythical tone, thanks to the haka— a Maori war dance—that the players performed before each game.

Miranda waved at a table of several people in a corner booth, and he followed her. Two women, a little girl and a man sat there, and the man rose immediately as James and Miranda approached. "Everyone," Miranda said, "this is James Marquez, from Albuquerque."

"How do you do," the man said, a curiously old-fashioned greeting James had not heard in a long time. He was quite tall, with a long braid and the uniform of a tribal cop. Now *this* guy, James thought, looked Indian. "Josh Mad Calf," the cop said. "Good to meet you."

James gave a nod, taking the proffered hand. Strong, straightforward grip. Intelligent eyes.

"These are my sisters," Miranda said, gesturing first toward a curvy, pretty blonde. "Juliet is engaged to Josh, and Desi—" she indicated the other, a woman with serious dark eyes, and the care-worn hands of a woman who worked with the land or animals or both "—is the one in so much trouble."

"Hello," he said, assessing each one. Juliet was sharp, an observer, her index finger tapping as she checked him out. Desi was weary, with soft bluish shadows beneath her eyes. Not as pretty as he would have expected for the charming, good-looking Claude, though there was a Sophia Loren appeal about her, all breasts and hair and sultry eyes. With a quirk of an eyebrows he took in all three sisters. "Wow. Neopolitan."

The brunette scowled. "As in ice cream?"

Miranda laughed, and the sound drew his attention once again. Such an earthy, sensual sound. "Chocolate, vanilla, and strawberry! I love it!" Seeing that her sister was not quite as amused, she rolled her eyes. "C'mon, Desi, lighten up! It's a joke. Remember jokes?"

"I apologize," James said. "It was inappropriate, but I didn't mean to be offensive." His attention caught on the little girl, with her black shiny hair and solemn dark eyes. She obviously belonged to the cop.

James said, "Hello. You must be about five, huh?"

She blinked, her mouth unsmiling. "I don't talk to strangers."

"Ah. Good."

A man, big as a bear, with the springy curls of an islander, came into the area. "Hey, mate," he said, extending a tattooed arm, "You must be the man, eh? I'm Tamati Neville. Everybody calls me Tam."

"James Marquez."

"Do they call you Jimmy?"

"Not really."

Tam grinned. "All right then. Sit down, what can I get you?"

"Just water, please."

"He's in training," Miranda said. "But I'll have a nice juicy margarita."

Tam said, "Are you running the Mariposa 50?"

"Yes."

"Good on ya."

The blonde—Juliet?—said, "Don't sit down yet, you guys. Glory and I are going to move over to another table while you talk about all this stuff."

"I'm not a baby!" Glory protested.

"Nobody said you were," Juliet said calmly. "It's icky stuff, though, and I don't want to hear it, either. 'Kay?"

"All right." She scooted out, carefully skirting around James, not even allowing her braid to touch him.

Miranda slid into the booth first, and James moved in behind her. The slippery faux leather of the booth rubbed static into her hair, and long tendrils stuck to the back of the seat in a fan. He pointed it out to her. "Looks like something in the ocean, doesn't it?"

"It does!" She used one finger to gather it and pull it back to her. "Have enough room?"

James nodded. Flipping open his notebook, he pulled his glasses from his pocket and put them on.

"Wish I could run again," the Maori—Tam—said. "I busted up my knee a few years ago and can't run like that anymore, but I miss it."

"I've never run this one," James said, "but it has a great reputation."

"We're counting on you, mate, to figure out who killed this sorry bastard. Get my girl—" he gripped Desi's shoulder "—out of this kettle of hot water she's stewing in, eh?"

"I'm going to do my best," James said. "Let me just go over the basic facts quickly, so we're all on the same page, all right?" Everyone nodded. "Claude was found on the reservation on the night of October 16. He was shot to death with a single bullet. The last person who officially saw him was a casino employee who watched him kiss his girlfriend—sorry—goodbye."

"So far so good," Desi said. "And really, if you stop

to apologize over every tawdry bit of this, we'll be here all day. You don't have to tiptoe with me."

He liked her, liked the directness of her gaze, the steadiness of her voice. "Okay. It looks bad for you, honestly. You have motive, weapon and opportunity. Add to that the fact that when a member of a love triangle is murdered its nearly always one of the other members who did it, and you fit like Cinderella's glass slipper."

"Right. Don't forget that I threatened to kill him in front of about twenty people, too."

James let himself smile slightly. "There's that, too."

"I didn't kill him," she said.

He met her eyes. "All right."

"Not that I didn't have some pretty brutal torture fantasies going, but I wouldn't kill him."

"So who else wanted him dead?"

Next to him, Miranda snorted softly, "Who didn't?"

He glanced over. She caught his eye, and it seemed they shared one moment of something secret. He looked back to his notes, flipped one page up. "Tell me if I miss anyone—developers, a different jilted lover— since I gather Christie Lundgren wasn't his first affair?"

"Right," Deşi said. "I don't know how many, though."

"Somebody knows," James said. "Did he have a good friend in town?"

"No. Only women."

James tapped the end of the pen against the page. "It might also be someone in the art world, or someone he double-crossed in some deal we don't know about."

He raised his head. "I know there was a big story about the developers who want your land for the aquifer, but I really doubt they're responsible for Claude's death."

Josh turned his lips downward. "You must have reasons."

"Well, it looks like a crime of passion, which can be staged, but a professional would be more thorough. This was pretty sloppy in a lot of ways—any number of places the killer could have been seen or caught."

Desi raised her eyebrows. "I never thought of that."

James asked, "Desi, can you give me Claude's story? How did you meet?"

"We were in the Peace Corps in Peru."

"Where did he grow up?"

"Mostly Denver, I think. He was born on the res, but then his parents divorced and his mother went to stay with an aunt in Denver."

"And he was Navajo?" James frowned at the page, his hand poised with a pen above the page.

"Yes."

"Do you know what town? What clan? Did he have people he stayed in contact with?"

"Bitter root clan, I think," Desi said. "And I think he said he was born near Tuba, but he really wasn't a reservation kind of guy. He never really lived there." She took a sip of her coffee. "His mother died when he was thirteen and he was in the streets for a while, then he ended up in foster care and went to Europe."

"Europe?" Tam said, "Is that how he knows Renate?"

Desi looked blank. "Renate?"

"The art dealer from Manhattan, remember?"

"Oh. Right." Desi waved a hand. "He always called her *katzchen*. Which I think might be kitten in German. They met when he was a teen. Somewhere in Bavaria, I think, and she came over here not long after he came back to the States."

A rippling of intuition moved on the back of James's neck. "Who is this? An art dealer?"

"I met her," Miranda said, her voice startlingly low and sexy. "I think I called you when I saw some of Claude's paintings up in a gallery in Soho. She had a lot of his work, and she had a showing a few months after Claude was murdered. That's what started the media frenzy over the winter."

James wrote a couple of notes to himself. "I'd like to find out more about her and her connection to the victim. Desi, if you can find anything with the addresses Claude lived at in Denver, or family members in Tuba City, that might be helpful."

She frowned slightly. "I'm not sure I know where you're going with that."

Josh spoke. "You think he might not have been who he said he was."

"Possible."

"Never looked Navajo to me," Josh said.

"Right." He looked around the table. "Anyone have any other ideas?"

"While you're looking into Renate, look into her connection with Elsa Franz," Josh said. "That was the other weird connection, two accented women with the same last name."

"Who is she?"

"A model, married to one of the developers now, Bill Biloxi."

James scribbled it all down. "What else? Who else?"

"Alice Turner," Desi said. "The dentist's wife. I think he had an affair with her, and she spearheaded a lot of political activity after he died. Trying to boycott the veterinary clinic and that kind of thing."

James wrote the name down. Drew an arrow up to the art dealer and a question mark—*connection?* "Did the value of Claude's paintings go up after he died?"

"Quadrupled," Miranda said. "At least."

He glanced down at her, suddenly aware of her thigh resting against his. His *tired* thigh. He closed his notebook, tucked the pen through the spiral at the top. "It's been a long day," he said. "I'm going to head back to my hotel and get some rest."

"Sure, mate?" Tam said. "Let us feed you some lamb stew. Good for your racing, I guarantee it."

"All right. But let the little one come back and we can talk about other things. Someone is getting married. Is that you?"

"No," Desi said, though she had a shine in her eyes when she looked at Tam. He reached over and tenderly covered her belly with his big hand.

"She won't marry me till she's in the clear, though

she's got me as the baby's guardian," he said, "so I'm counting on you, mate."

James nodded. "I'll do my best."

Chapter 4

Later that evening, Miranda dozed on the couch as she waited for Juliet to bring cups of decaffeinated coffee for them to drink. A big stack of envelopes and stamps and pens littered the table, and a John Wayne movie from the fifties—they all looked alike to her—played on the movie channel. Miranda couldn't motivate herself enough to change it.

"Here we go," Juliet sang, carrying a tray of cups and pitchers into the room. "Come sit over here at the table."

Miranda blinked and stood up. "I'm sleepy," she said.

"Probably the margaritas at dinner."

"Maybe." She shrugged.

"It was a lot of alcohol, sis. Is something bothering you?"

"It was two. Over two *hours*. With food." She rolled her eyes.

"And something before that. A beer?"

"Don't be so L.A."

"What does that mean?"

"All into the recovery scene, where all drinking is dangerous. Nobody just enjoys themselves anymore." Miranda glared at her sister, five years her senior. It was time both her sisters realized that she was an adult. "I really don't need your help in monitoring my drinking. I'm an adult. I'm not driving. I'm technically here to celebrate a wedding, and if I want some drinks, I'll have them."

"Touch a nerve, did I?"

Miranda sighed. "I don't know. Maybe."

Juliet raised an eyebrow, passing the sugar. "It's one thing when you have *a* drink. It's another when you slam them down to shut something out. What's bugging you?"

"I was living in Europe for almost a year, you know. They don't fret about drinking there, trust me. And don't even get me started on the New York scene. All people ever do is go for drinks."

Exasperated, Juliet said, "Miranda, stop talking to me like that. I'm your sister. I know you." She stirred milk into her own coffee and then tugged her hair back into a ponytail, that was, as everything was with Juliet, adorable. "Something is bothering you. Is it Mom and Dad's arrival?"

"No." Miranda waved a hand. There were things her

sisters didn't know about their parents, but there was no point to getting into any of it now. "I'll live with it." With a tiny spoon, she measured out superfine sugar and stirred it, watching the bowl of the spoon surface now and then like a fish in murky water.

"Is it Desi's trial?"

"No, I really don't think she's going to go to jail. I can't believe a fair world—"

The phone rang. Juliet answered it, and just as she said hello, Miranda had an intuition over who it would be. She mouthed, *I'm not here,* and waved her hands in front of her throat to gesture the same thing.

Juliet gave her an odd glance, but she dutifully said, "I'm sorry, she's not available right now. May I take a message?" She picked up a pen, and wrote something on a notebook alongside the phone. "Thanks. I'll let her know you called." The caller said something on the other end of the phone. "All right. Bye." She put the phone in the cradle and handed Miranda the slip of paper. "He wants you to call him."

Miranda looked down at the name and number. A dozen dizzying memories rushed through her, redolent with woodsmoke and spring and the crispness of mountain air.

"Curses," she said, and let her hand fall to her lap, suddenly feeling a slight headache from all the alcohol this evening. "Why is it so hard for all of us to tell each other what we are really feeling?"

"Humans, you mean?"

"No, me and you and Desi."

"Oh, I don't know," Juliet said with more than a little sarcasm. "Maybe it's being raised by two narcissists."

Miranda nodded. Pressure burned in her chest, a tangle of unexpressed anger, hurt, love. She had not told anyone about her intense, painful love affair with Max Boudrain. It was too humiliating.

Juliet reached over and touched her hand. "It's okay to tell me anything, Miranda."

What if I said, Miranda thought, *that your father is not my father? That our parents have been having affairs all of our lives?* "I bet I could think of things you wouldn't want to hear."

"Maybe I wouldn't like it, but I'd still listen." She paused. "There's nothing you can say that would make me stop loving you, that's for sure."

Stung, Miranda bowed her head. "It's nothing like that. I just had a dumb love affair and got a broken heart, and he's here. In Mariposa. I saw him this afternoon."

"Is that *the* Max Boudrain?" Juliet asked, touching the paper with one index finger. "The skier who did so well at Turin?"

"Yeah." Miranda's mouth twisted into a wry grimace. "I should have known better."

"Because he's a skier?"

"All of it," Miranda said wearily. "Beautiful and European and talented and—" She waved a hand dismissively. "All of it," she repeated. "It takes a saint to resist the women who fawn over a man like that."

"And I take it Max wasn't a saint?"

"Well, I don't know." She tossed hair out of her eyes. "The thing is, we didn't really have that kind of relationship. I met him at a dinner party and we had this wild affair for a few months, and then we parted company."

"Friendly terms?"

"I guess."

Juliet tucked her foot beneath her knee. "Tell me about him, Mirrie. All of it."

Miranda sipped her coffee, and opened the mental box where she'd shoved her memories of Max, hurry-scurry, where they'd stop giving her so much pain. They spilled out on the floor, moments of blue and green and vivid pink, the colors of the Mediterranean. "I went to Nice for a show, and to do some research for a new project. Have you been there?"

"Never got further south than Paris, I'm afraid."

"It's slightly seedy and too colorful and has this air of too much drink—but it's so beautiful. Beautiful. The blue Mediterranean, the palms, the flowers spilling out of window boxes and growing in ditches and waste places…" She shook her head. "There are beautiful humans in the streets and on the beaches and sitting in the sidewalk cafés." She'd been sketching the scene with her hand, and now dropped it to her lap. "And there was Max, all toned and tanned from the season, his body so big and strong and graceful."

"Mmm."

"And he wasn't American. There was that slightly delicious frisson of his accent whenever he talked to me. That worldly sense of everything—" She shook her head.

"Didn't Mother and Daddy go to Nice some summers?"

"Yes. Nice and Zurich—and I think sometimes they went to Cape Town for some reason." A shrug. "Hang out with all their soignée friends, rent a house and drink all summer long on the beaches talking poetry and science."

Miranda paused, fingering the edge of the paper with Max's name and telephone number, lost in reveries. Twice, she'd been dragged along—one year when she was too young to go to camp with the other sisters, and another year when she'd had bronchitis severely through the winter and even Carol Rousseau was worried about leaving her child. It was thought the Nice summer would heal her.

No California bungalow for them, of course. That would be so left coast, so not their thing. Blue bloods, the Rousseaus. Or at least their mother was. Their father—that would be Paul, the poet father, not the natural father Miranda had never known, was the son of a factory worker in Maine. But he did have some family in the Nice area, so they had their connections.

"We have a cousin in Nice," she said now. "Henri."

"I remember him! He came to stay when you were very little. He's maybe ten years older than I am?"

"Right. I stopped to visit him, and he and his very lovely wife hosted a supper for me in the way only the French can do, with a thousand courses spread over six hours and wine flowing, and everyone talking and laughing, and Max was there, a friend of the family.

And we sat together, and he spoke English and French both, so he could smooth things on the conversational front."

"Wow," Juliet said softly, and leaned forward with a tiny smile edging her lips. "You're such a good storyteller."

"Oh, it's nothing," Miranda said. "Comes from having to sparkle at gallery openings."

"I don't care, I'm enthralled. Tell me more."

"He was so charming." Remembering, Miranda felt the stab in her chest that she'd been running from these past six months. "He had direct, beautiful eyes—not quite blue, not quite gray, not quite green." She paused, surprised at the detail of her memories, what she'd resolutely refused to let into her daily life. "Sometimes, those eyes seemed they were the color of steel. Sometimes, they were the vivid blue of the sea. How could she *not* have fallen for a man with eyes like that? "He made me feel beautiful, which is kind of rare for me."

"Oh, Miranda, how can you say that?"

"Lots of reasons," she snorted. "I'm too tall. I'm redheaded, which you either love or don't love, and more people fall in the not-love category. White skin, the white of a carp belly. Never tans. Ever. And—" she raised a finger "—I'm as flat an egg. A fried egg, not an ostrich egg like you and Desi."

"You took after Dad's side of the family," Juliet said, grinning. "The French side. Desi and I inherited the English bosom."

"And it was in France that I met Max, so maybe

that's why he thought I was so beautiful, or made me feel that way. Whatever." She took a breath. "It was a very intense affair for about two months. We went all over Europe, and then, just like that—" she snapped her fingers "—it was over. He said he didn't want to see me anymore. He had a busy career and there wasn't time for a big romance."

"Ow! That had to hurt. I'm sorry!"

"It did, but I'm mostly over it. But I hated running into him today. I could tell he was going to do the big apology thing and I'll fall right under his spell all over again, and I'm just not going to go there, you know?"

"Smart decision. Nothing says you have to call him back."

"You know who he's staying with, though? This is important: Christie Lundgren."

Juliet scowled. "That woman. She's just got it in for Desi."

"Well, look at it from her side, Juliet."

"I guess." She frowned. "I just want this fixed so we can have a big, happy party on my wedding!"

Miranda laughed. "It's all about you, after all."

"It is! It's my wedding!"

"I know. And I'm actually pretty excited. Josh is fantastic."

Juliet nodded, put a hand to her heart. "He is."

"I like Tam, too. He's besotted with our Desi."

"He's great."

Miranda wondered if she'd ever find a mate as her sisters had. Maybe she didn't want it. Maybe she didn't believe in it on some level, even if she wanted to. To distract herself she asked, "Didn't you get some more flower choices today?"

"I did! Do you want to see them?"

"Absolutely."

Juliet jumped up and brought back a series of photos with various bouquets.

Miranda pushed everything else out of her mind and focused on her sister's joy. "God, it *is* great to see you so happy," she said. "Especially after—"

"The rape? You can say it. I'll never be glad it happened, but coming here, finding Josh and Glory and the town has been very healing."

"Will you have babies together?"

"I certainly hope so."

"I can be an auntie."

"You will be anyway."

"Glory? Yeah, but I want more."

"And Desi, too—don't forget."

"That's right. It's just so new still, I haven't gotten use to it. Do Mother and Daddy know?"

"No, and she doesn't want them to. She's going to be four months along by the wedding, and we're having some trouble thinking how to dress her."

"Does she think she can have a baby without them ever knowing?"

"No, I'm sure she doesn't. It's just for now—she'd rather not tell Mother and have to listen to all her crap."

"In person," Miranda acknowledged. "I can find something for her to wear, I betcha, either in town or the Internet, then fix it up a little. Does anybody have a sewing machine?"

"You're a godsend, Mirrie. Yes—Helene Mad Calf has a sewing machine. I'm sure she'll loan it to us." She stood up. "Why don't you get to bed now. You look beat."

"I need my rest to deal with our parents," Miranda agreed.

She kissed her sister's head and made her way to the spare bedroom. As she undressed and brushed her teeth and washed her face, as she rubbed heavy cream into her hands and feet and light oil into her arms and legs, she found herself thinking not of Max at all.

It was the piercing, see-all dark eyes of James Marquez that hung on the screen of the day, eyes that moved from twinkling to somber to sultry to teasing in seconds. A man of great passions and fierceness, but also laughter and lightness.

If she painted him, he would seem severe if his eyes were not done just right. She rubbed her face on a towel—someone had told her it was good to rub your skin vigorously to stimulate the cells or something—and found a soft rippling on her nape.

James, it said. She had never met anyone like him.

Alone in the thirties-style bathroom with its line of lime-green tiles round the room, Miranda was surprised to realize how much she'd noticed about the detective. His strong, dark hands with their clean, oval nails. The scattering of dark hair over his forearm, the fullness of his luscious mouth.

What was his story, anyway? She wondered why

he'd turned away from the priesthood. A woman, maybe? A loss of faith?

She wrinkled her nose in the mirror, rubbing her finger over the dusting of pale freckles on her nose. A man who had wanted to be a priest was probably way out of her league, too straight, too prim to deal with a woman who'd—

Never mind.

He just wasn't the kind of man she was ordinarily drawn to, and yet, the little hairs on her nape rustled when she thought of him. Here she was, feeling that need to review their conversation, review the sound of his voice, revisit the look of his mouth.

Crawling between the cool, crisp sheets in her sister's guest room, Miranda lay down and let her body go, closed her eyes and felt some free part of her spirit dance over the details of his face, that cheekbone, that eyebrow, one more time.

Don't even go there, she told herself. Just don't.

At 5:00 a.m., James loosely jogged toward the gondola that ran over the mountain. So early in the morning, there were not many people about, but he did pass a handful of runners in training, and a couple of others who might have just been out to take their daily exercise.

At the top of the mountain, he got out of the gondola and gave a nod to the boy who opened the door for him.

"Training for the 50?" the boy asked, nodding at James's singlet and tiny running shorts.

"I am."

"Have a good run."

James lifted a hand and walked out to an area that in summer was a ski area. And although he'd grown up in the Sangre de Cristo mountains of New Mexico, although he'd run on mountain trails in the past, in spite of both those things, he stopped for one moment in purest gratitude. The peaks of the San Juans rose in ancient craggy splendor, the rocks faintly pink in the crystal clear dawn. Spills of trees, aspen and pine, tumbled down toward the valley far below, the blocks of houses looking like something false, cardboard toys laid out for children. He stood in the cool morning, letting the fresh mountain air fill his body, then exhaled, and jogged on a trail that led to the north.

To begin, he said the rosary, all fifty decades, chanting them on his fingers as he loosened up. He'd run for a long time with beads around his wrist, but took enough ribbing he learned to do it on his hands. Faith was a private matter, between himself and his Maker. He felt no wish to defend his position or convert others to his way of thinking. If he'd learned one thing during his quest, it was that there were many paths to the divine. His was his own.

This morning, he sought wisdom, guidance for his intuition and intellect. Intellect said Desi had likely killed Claude, no matter how much everyone wanted to believe otherwise, and intuition said she had not done it, that there was a darker evil afoot here. The land Desi and Claude had shared was worth one hell of a lot of money, and someone stood to make barrels more from it. That was as much a motive as a marriage gone foul.

Claude had obviously collected a number of lovers. James needed to find out how many, where they were, what his love history was. Someone knew. It could be that some jilted woman had just grown tired of him taking yet another lover.

His breath came more harshly as he ran a slight grade up a ridge, and sweat now started beading along his brow, but there was good rhythm in his movements this morning, a good stride even at what he guessed was nearly eleven thousand feet. He'd done a lot of altitude training in preparation for this race, and he felt it paying off now. The oxygen at such altitudes was about two-thirds of what it was at sea level. It took the body time to get used to that.

Once he'd grown acclimated, he ran easily, without much thought to his feet or lungs, just the steady, steady rhythm that could carry him many long miles.

One part of his brain was cataloging features—the sharp incline alongside a meadow that led—happily— to a long, relatively straight stretch where he could rest and recover. Through the trees to cool down, then over a rocky, difficult stretch that required close attention.

The rest of his brain moved the puzzle pieces of the case around, then slid sideways toward Miranda. He drew his thoughts back to the case, to making a mental list of what needed doing today, then sneaked back toward the woman. He resolutely thought of the race, of who his strongest competitors might be, of what things he should prepare for, how to eat and sleep.

In memory, he heard the sound of her laughter, low and hearty. He pondered the mysterious attachment to the skier. Lovingly reviewed the stunning sight of her breasts clasped by pale lace.

He refocused on his feet, into the tightening muscles along his right quadriceps muscle, tiring because of the of the trail. He breathed into it, imagined cooling blue gel filling the area, and it eased slightly.

Then to the case.

Who killed Claude Tsosie? Who were the possibilities? He listed them in his mind, in a neat line: Desi. Developers. Jilted lover. Someone in the art world.

Any others he might have overlooked? Ah. A lover's *partner*—husband or lover of a woman who'd fallen for Claude. Yes.

He had his work cut out for him, that much was true, and unless he could uncover the real killer, there was one thing absolutely certain: Desdemona Rousseau was going to go to jail.

A sudden scrambling sounded in the forest to his left, and James jerked his head around. A fox, fluffy red and beautiful, landed on the trail as if he'd fallen from a ledge or just tumbled down the hillside. James froze. The fox, slightly bewildered, made a complaining noise and jumped to its feet, as if cursing some bad driver.

James chuckled and the fox whipped his head around. For one long second, they stared at each other, animal and man. Its eyes were black and shiny, the nose

long and sharp. James could see in great detail the ruff
of fur on his chest, many of the individual hairs, had
enough time to notice the whiskers, the tiny hand-paws.
Then it seemed to realize it was staring at a *man*—an
enemy!—and dashed across the trail, chattering, its
thick tail the last thing to disappear into a stand of low
bushes.

Miranda.

James let go of a breath and laughed aloud, waving
a hand at the heavens. He was smart enough to see a
sign when one arrived. He would not ignore the skittish,
redheaded Miranda as he'd half intended. He would
pursue her, *Zorrorita,* little fox.

And then he pursed his lips and looked back over his
shoulder. Maybe the fox meant to tell him more than
that. Maybe Miranda knew something that would help
solve the case. Maybe it was something she didn't even
realize she knew.

Or maybe, he was just a fox.

Chapter 5

There was a murder to solve and her parents coming to town and an old boyfriend to deal with, Miranda thought, putting on her big black sunglasses, but there was also a wedding to finish planning. Clutching a list in her right hand, she headed out into the village to see if she could find a dress for Desi, or at least something that could be altered or brightened for her.

Last night, Miranda and Juliet had gone through the last of the flower choices and settled on a mix of blue and green hydrangeas, calla lilies in cream and pure white, and roses in a rainbow of colors and shapes. The florist would fly the blooms in from Denver the night before and make everything up in the tents they were setting up outside the hotel where the ceremony would be held. The cake was ordered, the party favors chosen. Juliet's dress was purchased, altered minutely, and now—draped in fine plastic film and tissue paper—awaited the big day. Miranda had her own dress, one Juliet had approved, and their mother almost certainly would not, a vintage Woodstock-era beauty she'd found on eBay.

All that remained was to find something for Desi, who had never been tremendously fond of dresses, but was also pregnant, extraordinarily busty—even more so in pregnancy—and broad shouldered. A hard fit, but Miranda had confidence in her inner eye.

As a nod to the usual sources, she stopped in a couple of boutiques along Black Diamond Boulevard, and found some charming and odd things, as one did in such places. She lingered over a soft pink twenties-style dress with a filmy overdress, and again over a sleek brown silk that would have set off her creamy skin, but moved on after some consideration. Neither was right for Desi.

Instead she headed outside and opened the phone book to find out if there were any secondhand shops. She found two: the St. Vincent de Paul's thrift shop, which was right around the corner from the casino, and Rita's Remnants, on Second. Headed for the first one, she found herself humming happily. A butterfly, black with an edging of blue iridescence, landed on a bank of wild purple monarda that grew in a clump by the edge of a redbrick garage. Miranda pulled out the tiny digital camera she always carried and leaned in to snap some shots, intrigued by the combination of textures and colors—scalloped, delicate wings, repetitive blooms, the hard edges of the building. Even some quartz, glistening white, in the background.

"Fantastic," she said aloud, lowering the camera. The eye caught things the camera could not; the mind made connections a machine never knew.

"Yes, it is," said a voice nearby.

Miranda didn't quite startle, but there was a rush of that...whatever down her nape when she raised her head to see James Marquez leaning against the building. He'd obviously been watching her, and had come from a run—he wore a paper-thin singlet and a tiny pair of royal-blue running shorts and running shoes stained with red earth at the toes. His legs were the color of cinnamon, corded with lean muscle.

"Hi," she said, finally, dragging her gaze up to his face. Which also gave her that slight zing of pleasure— the startling passion of his mouth in the midst of those angles, the dark and teasing eyes, that fall of licorice hair on his brow. "Have you been running or are you going?"

"Just back," he said, crossing his arms, which were not as blade thin as she would have imagined, but respectably toned. He smiled. "I'll keep my distance."

"That's all right. I don't mind honest sweat." She pointed to the insects feeding on flower nectar. "Do you know what kind of butterfly that is?"

"Mourning cloak," he said. "They're famous around here. The shrine on the mountain is Our Lady of the Butterflies."

"A shrine?"

"Yes." He raised one eyebrow. "You should visit."

Miranda grinned. "Trying to reform my wicked shrine-building ways, are you?"

"You would find it beautiful."

Instinctively she raised her camera and shot a photo of him before she even looked in the viewfinder. And when she did, he met her eyes steadfastly, the blackness both frank and mysterious. Miranda nodded. "I'll think about it." Tucking the camera away, she tossed her hair over her shoulder. "I'd better go. I'm on a mission."

He nodded, but didn't immediately move. "I like it that you wear skirts."

Miranda felt his gaze on her bare legs, almost as clearly as if he were skimming a hand over her shins, over her knee, lightly up her thigh. She swallowed. "Um. Thanks."

His gaze remained fixed on her legs, traveled down to her feet, clad in a pair of turquoise wedges with rhinestones. "And you paint your toenails."

He said it slowly, raised his eyes and she had the sense that he was toying with her, but it was not the toying of a housecat batting round a mouse. A lion, a tiger. No, not quite…a big cat. She found herself looking at his mouth again, and her nipples suddenly straightened, as if that mouth was on them, as if his tongue—

She frowned and took a step back, rattled slightly. "Okay, whatever," she said, attempting to cloak herself in derision as a modern woman was wont to do.

But her heel stuck in the crack of the sidewalk, stuck hard, and she was thrown off balance. Her foot slipped in the shoe, and she lurched sideways, tugged the shoe free and pitched right into his strong grip.

His scent ripped violently into her, piercing her body in a dozen ways, all at once. It rushed over her neck and shoulders, down her spine, causing a ripple of lavalike heat over her back; it dived right through her nostrils to the back of her tongue, through her gut and into her belly, and lower still, like a fist, into her sex. She made a soft noise, a gasp of surprise, and gripped his hands and—almost against her will—sucked in a great lungful of his sweat, hot and spicy, clean and sharp. Not a smell she should like, but it swelled every molecule of her body, and she leaned infinitesimally closer to the sleek, slick skin only inches away from her mouth, her tongue, and gripped his bicep, smooth and hot beneath her fingers, and it made her think of other flesh, rigid and ready to plunge into her, dive—

"*Madre,*" he whispered, a soft curse.

Miranda realized that he could see down her blouse—as he had yesterday, and hadn't she sort of planned this, hoped she would meet him?—to the thin lace clasping her breasts. She certainly could feel the rigidness of nipples shoving at that lace, and could only imagine what he saw.

And he, too, was aroused, the weight of his sex filling—

Miranda looked away, her face burning. What was *wrong* with her? "I'm sorry…I'm…this is…"

"You all right now?"

"Yes. Yeah." She nodded. Shifted her weigh to demonstrate, brushed hair off her face. Which was probably as red as a tomato.

"I need your help with something," he said. "I'll find you later today."

"All right." Miranda waved a hand toward town. "I'll be around. You have my cell number."

For one more moment, he stared at her, his eyes unreadable, then lifted a hand and ran toward the top of the hill.

In other circumstances, Miranda might have let her knees buckle. Instead she walked shakily toward a bar of shade nearby the building and leaned there, waving a hand. It was the heat, she told herself. That was all.

After a minute, her limbs felt normal and she looked up the hill the way he'd run. *I'll find you later today.* Maybe she'd do better to make sure he didn't find her.

Miranda couldn't find anything for Desi at the St. Vincent de Paul's, or the secondhand shop. None of the boutiques had had anything. She'd even combed the weekly paper for garage sales, and looked for a costume shop where she might be able to buy something to make over.

No luck.

Frustrated, tired and thirsty, she ducked into ReNew, the coffee shop she so enjoyed. The faint smell of patchouli mingled with freshly baked blueberry scones and the dense siren call of freshly ground coffee beans.

Miranda halted just inside the door and inhaled deeply. "Heaven," she said.

Sarah, a sturdy blond ski bum with bright blue eyes in her tanned face, grinned. "Nothing like the smell of fresh coffee."

"I'll have a latte," Miranda said. "And whatever scone you think is best today."

"You got it," Sarah said. Her voice was low and cracked, a sexy sound that made her seem more worldly. As she measured coffee with efficient movements, she inclined her head. "You're looking bummed, lady. Everything all right?"

"Yeah. Well, aside from my sister being up for murder and all."

"That sucks, dude."

Miranda nodded, wandering over to the CDs while she waited. Something with a faintly Persian sound played on the overhead speakers. Above the racks was a scarf, beaded and gossamer, and a light flashed in Miranda's brain. "A sari!" she said aloud, snapping her fingers.

"I'm sorry?" Sarah asked, revealing her upper middle class roots.

"My sister needs a dress for the wedding. I haven't been able to find anything decent. A sari would be perfect."

The girl poured milk into a pitcher. "Isn't the wedding in, like, a week?"

"Yeah, that's a problem. Maybe I can find somebody to deliver."

"They probably have something in Denver." She put

the milk beneath the steamer and raised her chin toward a bank of computers against the wall. "Check the Internet."

The only other person on the computers was a boy with a stocking cap and grimy fingernails, a large backpack at his knee. He typed in some language Miranda didn't recognize, not quite German. Maybe Danish. She slid into a seat and brought up the Internet and found three places that sold saris in the Denver area. She drank her latte and gobbled the scone, and punched the numbers to each one into her cell phone.

The first one was not interested in trying to get a sari to Mariposa within two days, and there was no answer at the second place, but on her third try, Miranda found a man who was more than willing to work with her, figure out what she wanted, and send someone down with a couple of different things for Desi to try. All for a price, of course, but that was one of the things the sisters really never had to worry about, was it? Money.

She asked for three saris to be brought down, one in blue, one in pink, one in yellow. Buoyed, she hung up and wandered around the shop, picking up things here and there to accent a sari as wedding attire, a pair of silver earrings, a silver bracelet with bells, a silver barrette for Desi's thick, beautiful hair. Carrying her things to the counter, she hummed a light tune.

A man came around the corner, blond and hale and sturdy. Miranda started, glanced over her shoulder for a place to run, but she was trapped. She swore under her breath. *Damn, damn, damn.*

"Good morning, Miranda," said Max, his voice elegantly accented, beautiful.

"Hi, Max." She spilled her goods on the counter. "Are you enjoying your stay?"

"Yes." He gestured toward the tables. "Will you sit? Have a cup of coffee?"

"Oh, I'm sorry. I've got to run." She looked at her bare wrist. "I have to take these things to my sister."

Sarah was standing very still, her blue eyes blisteringly blue. "Aren't you Max Boudrain? The gold-medal skier?"

He glanced at her, dismissively, gave a curt, "Yes," then turned his focus back to Miranda. "Only a little while? A few moments."

Miranda scowled at him. "Max, I'd like you to meet Sarah. She's living here because her life is skiing. I bet she'd love your autograph." Whipping a black pen from her purse, she gave it to him, along with a postcard from the counter.

One side of his mouth lifted. "Trade?"

"Sign it, Max."

He lifted a thick brown-blond brow. "All right." He looked at the girl. "Sarah with an H?"

Miranda's phone rang, and she glanced at the screen. "I'll be right back," she said to the girl, and headed out to take the call. "Hi, James," she said, flipping open the phone.

"Hi, Miranda. I'm standing here across the street from ReNew."

She whirled around, putting a hand up to shade her

eyes. He stood in a fall of thick shadows, his face made hard in very dark sunglasses. That odd little shimmer went through her belly. "I'm here!" she waved.

He raised a hand. "I wonder if you'd do me a favor?"

"I'll try."

"Have a cup of coffee with your old boyfriend. See if you can find out anything about Christie and her feelings for Claude. Just—whatever."

Miranda's chest got tight. "Uh…James…I—"

"It might help, Miranda. Remember the point is to clear your sister's name."

"Right. Okay. Shall I find you somewhere later?"

"I have to interview some people and I'm going to sniff around the casino a bit. Call me when you're done."

"Ten-four," she said, one side of her mouth lifting. "Or is that 'Roger'?"

"Over and out, good buddy," he said, and raised a hand.

Miranda spun on her heel and went back inside. "Okay, Max," she said, "let's have that coffee. But you have to buy me a scone, too." She'd just had one, but two in one day wouldn't kill her.

"Of course," he said. He touched the small of her back. "Two," he said to Sarah.

They settled beside the window, paper cups in their hands. "How have you been, Miranda?"

"All right." She shrugged. "You know me. I land on my feet."

"You look wonderful."

Miranda forced a smile. "So do you, as always." And it was true, she had to admit, but there was a dark stone of resentment or resistance in her as she looked at him. A wisp of a French love song brushed through the hollows of her heart, and she straightened. "How's your leg?"

A shadow moved over his mouth. "It is healing, but more slowly than I expected. In truth, I came here to see a physical therapist who is known to help with difficult cases."

"So it's serious?"

"It could be."

"What happened?"

"It was so foolish," he said, peering into his coffee. "I was on a yacht and a wave came and I stumbled on the stairs. Twisted my knee."

Miranda couldn't help it—she laughed. "What did you tell the newspapers?"

His lips curled up in amused acknowledgment. "Training accident."

"Ah." Miranda wondered how to bring the conversation to Christie without seeming obvious.

"And you? You're here with the runner?"

Startled, she blinked up at him. "Runner? Oh, James. No. Not at all. He—ah." She made herself stop. Breathe. "I'm here to see my sisters. They both live here now. Didn't Christie fill you in?"

"No."

"She certainly seemed hostile enough."

Max took a slow sip of his coffee, settled the mug

before raising his gaze. "It seems you two are on opposite sides of a conflict, but I do not think that is true. One of the reasons I came to Mariposa is that the skiing community is concerned about her. She is a friend. She loved him—the one who was murdered. Claude, is it?"

"Right. My sister's late husband."

"Your sister's marriage was failing, yes?"

Miranda shrugged. "I have no idea. I was in Europe at the time."

His gaze raked her face. "Yes. I remember."

"And philanderers all say their marriages are in trouble."

"Yes, that's true. Christie is very young, however. Perhaps she thought it was genuine. For all we know, perhaps it was."

"Genuine? Claude? I doubt it." She didn't know how to get more information. Or what to even look for. How did investigators lead without tipping their hands?

Maybe it was just a matter of conversation. "Doesn't she usually live in Europe, too?"

"In Bavaria, which is where we met."

Bavaria. Why did that ring a bell? Miranda made a mental note of it. "What was she doing here to start with?"

"Training. She keeps a home here. How do you say it? A condo. The slopes are particularly good." He paused. "She met Claude at a hotel bar. He swept her off her feet."

Miranda sighed. "I know. I feel sorry for her, but her

lack of cooperation with the investigation might end up putting Desi in jail. I love my sister. She's in love and pregnant and her ex-husband was awful to her. *She* doesn't deserve this, either."

"Perhaps I can speak to her."

"Will you, Max?"

He reached over the table, took her hand. "Will you give me another chance?"

She pulled her hand from beneath his as hastily as if he were on fire. "No."

"I was a fool, Miranda. You frightened me. The fire frightened me. Haven't you thought of us since then?"

She stared at him so hard he bowed his head. Sunlight danced in the wheat thickness of his hair and a memory—quickly shoved away—trailed over her vision. Laughing on a Mediterranean beach, with the sound of a dozen languages in the air—

So romantic! It had all been so romantic. Had she been in love with Max, or with the pleasure of the story they could tell, the way her love affair could embroider her life.

Either way, he'd been cold in the way he'd cut it off. Her heart had been broken, and it didn't really matter whether it was broken over a man or a fantasy. The pain had been quite real.

"Yes," she said. "I've thought of it. The answer is no. I am happy to be your friend. There will be nothing else."

He swallowed. "Very well. I will still try to speak with Christie on your behalf." He stood. "I am sorry, Miranda, for everything."

She only nodded.

Chapter 6

While Miranda had coffee with her skier, James headed over to the casino. Claude had been gambling there with Christie just before he was murdered, and it seemed a logical place to see if anyone would talk to him. See if anyone had seen anything that should be remembered.

At midday on a Thursday, the casino still held a fair number of people, mostly stationed with zombie gazes at the slot machines, fingers pressing buttons, lights flashing. A few poker tables and blackjack hard cores played. It was mercifully smoke-free, and all the employees were Indian.

James wandered around getting the feel for things, then chose a bar at random and sat down with a stack of quarters in front of a video poker machine. A beefy Native man with long braids wrapped old-style in leather, approached and put a napkin down on the bar. "What can I get you?"

"Soda water with lime."

The man ambled over to the spigot, poured the soda. James played a few quarters, won a few, played another hand, won five bucks. "Huh," he said, and grinned at the bartender. "Beginner's luck, I guess."

"I guess."

He took a sip of the soda water, laid a five-dollar bill on the bar. The man's tag read *Bear*. "Bear, you worked here a long time?" James asked.

"Since it opened."

"You here the night the artist got murdered?"

"Yep." The dark eyes were hard. "You a reporter?"

"No. I'm working for his ex-wife, the one accused of killing him."

"Sure, Desi Rousseau. She's good people, man."

James nodded. "You see Claude that night?"

"He played blackjack. Lost a bundle, then won a bit. His girlfriend was with him."

"The skier. Christie Lundgren?"

Bear nodded. "He brought in a new one all the time. Dog."

"Yeah? Like you know any of the others?"

"Tourists, mainly. In town to ski or hike, you know? Out for a good time. Once in a while, he came with a German, and for a little while there, he was with that model. Elsa?"

"He sounds like a bastard."

"Lotta people coulda killed him, that's for sure."

"Where would you put your money?"

"The girlfriend, man."

"She's got an airtight alibi."

"Mebbe she put somebody up to it. They were fighting over Desi when they were here. I heard 'em."

"And if not her, who?"

"Some woman. A man would have just counted crow all over his sorry ass."

James laughed. "Chased him back to the res?"

Bear rolled his eyes. "Urban cowboy, man. Didn't know nothing about Navajo ways. My mom's Dineh. He didn't know nothing."

"Did you see Claude talking to anyone else that night?"

"He was always talking. The developer was here, and the model. They were all talking. Having a good time, looked like."

James's phone rang and he said, "Sorry. Gotta take this." He flipped the phone open and said, "Miranda. Talk to me."

"Not sure what I got, but I talked." Her voice sounded thin. "You want to meet me somewhere?"

"Come to the casino. I'll buy you a 7-Up."

"I just had coffee."

"Okay, where do you want to meet? Your call."

"I don't know, James. I don't know this town, either."

She sounded like a slightly cranky five-year-old,

and he smiled. "You know where the church is, don't you? It's right between us. Dead center of town. Go in and sit there in the cool and I'll find you."

"The church? I don't—"

"You'll like it, Miranda. Trust me."

She sighed. "Whatever. I'll see you there."

The day had grown hot. Miranda put on her sunglasses, and strolled down the upscale village streets of Mariposa feeling mysterious and beautiful, like Jackie O. The thought made her smile—and she felt her walk change, her spine grow straighter. Imagination was a powerful thing. Feeling like Jackie O, she *became* Jackie O on some level.

Imagination. Maybe that was what had been so appealing about her whirlwind love affair with Max. It had all been staged against the dashing backdrops of Nice and Austria, Paris and Zurich.

Just like her parents.

The thought startled her. Unpleasantly. Had she really imitated her narcissistic, annoying parents to that degree?

But hadn't they done exactly that—spun a fantasy of two worldly people who traveled and studied and cleverly hosted the wealthy, the brilliant, the talented?

With a sick sense of recognition, she yanked off her sunglasses, afraid to be anything like them at all. High altitude sunlight blasted her irises, and she winced and put the glasses back on. Jackie O, after all, had adopted the glasses in Greece, hadn't she?

Oh, what was wrong with wanting to be worldly? She'd dreamed of the faraway and exotic from the time she was a small girl and Desi read to her from the *Arabian Nights*. Everywhere seemed intriguing. All names exotic.

But—to return to the original thought—that slice of the exotic probably had contributed to her feelings for Max.

What was real? she thought. What was a fantasy spun out of some need?

And how could you tell the difference?

The church stood on a corner facing the San Juans, built of reddish sandstone at the turn of the century. A bell tower rose from one corner, and heavy steps led to arched wooden doors. To one side was a deep *nicho* sheltering a statue of Our Lady of Butterflies, a classic dark-skinned Madonna with black robes edged in blue, and butterflies lighting around her shoulders. A real butterfly rested on the statue's nose, and Miranda chuckled, pulling out her camera. Easing close, she focused on the shimmering wings and snapped the photo. Then again.

A low, softly accented voice said, "What are the chances, hmm?"

Miranda lowered the camera as if his voice did not disturb her in the slightest. "That a butterfly would land on a statue of Our Lady of Butterflies?"

"No," he said, and took a step to stand beside her, admiring the statue and the church. He smelled of herbal shampoo and clean skin, and she had a swift vision of that place in the middle of his chest, the shallow dent where ribs met. Dark, soft hair…her mouth—

She bent her head. "Then what?"

"That I would twice in one day find you while you were photographing butterflies." He smiled down at her, his eyes a dark chocolate, his lips full-cut and red and imminently kissable.

She shrugged, against him, against the lure of the visions. "I take photos all the time."

Unaccountably, he smiled. It was, she thought darkly, an awfully knowing smile for a man who was once almost a priest. "Let's go in, shall we? It's quite extraordinary," he gestured with one hand, "particularly given your interest in altars."

He stepped aside and Miranda climbed the steps, her feet tracing the worn spots where thousands of feet had gone before. It would be slippery in the rain or the snow. She pulled open the doors, and startled as something brushed by her face on its way into the church. A butterfly, then another.

The interior of the church was cool and smelled of dust and candles and rose incense. After the vivid brightness outside, Miranda couldn't see much at all, and pulled off her sunglasses.

"Oh!" she breathed. She halted for one long moment, the glasses in her hand, then drifted forward as if reeled in by the altar itself. As she caught the full spectrum of it, her mouth opened and she let go of a small, delighted laugh. "Oh!" she said again, and touched her heart.

The church itself was not large, just a classically designed cross with the chancel at the back and a single center aisle with old, dark, wooden pews to either side. Windows were cut high on the walls on either side, and they were set with earnest but not particularly well-done stained glass of biblical scenes.

But the altar was huge, wooden, with a dozen niches. The style was adamantly Spanish colonial, with carved flowers and cherubs and winding vines and mournful looking male faces. It had been well-cared for, with fresh paint on the orange and blue flowers and the white robes of the monks and the shining pink and orange robes of the Lady, her arms and head dancing with butterflies. Carved ones, painted carefully to resemble the local mourning cloaks, and real ones, their wings moving on currents of air as the Madonna smiled down kindly.

"It's spectacular," Miranda whispered, hungrily devouring details of color and proportion. "The niches are fantastic." It drew her closer and closer, her hands over her heart, camera forgotten. Bowls of flowers in single colors, orange marigolds, blue pincushion flowers and shell-pink roses, sat on a table before the altar. Racks of candles flickered.

James came quietly behind her. Miranda felt the heat of his body down her spine, pooling around her left shoulder blade, her hip. "Worth seeing?"

"It's much older than the church," she said with certainty. "Mexican, maybe 1800s?"

"Very good. It's Santa Fean, 1802." His voice resonated through her collarbone, into the thin cartilage of her outer ear. His breath touched her neck. Like a warm butterfly.

Miranda brushed the spot. "How do you know that?"

"It's famous," he said. "Carved by a priest who was known as an advocate for the Indians. He was killed eventually, under mysterious circumstances."

"I wish I could touch it."

"Let's find the priest. I'm sure it will be all right. You're an artist."

Standing before such a magnificent carving, Miranda knew the smallness of her art. "No, I play. *This* is art."

"You stay and admire it. I'll find the priest or someone to ask if we can touch it."

Miranda nodded, sinking into the first pew to absorb it. She put her tickling palms together, feeling a peculiar lure on her neck. What would it be like to create a real altar? In a Santa Fe importer's shop, she'd seen a collection of Tibetan altars, many of them ancient, and those had affected her this same way. She felt both humbled and inspired, challenged and enchanted.

So much love.

Which was why, of course, she could not ever create such a thing. She was too cynical.

James returned, smiling, and gestured for Miranda to approach the altar. "He said it would be fine, that we should be respectful and be careful of the candles."

"He did?"

"I know him," he admitted with a twinkle in his eye. "We were at seminary together."

"Ah. The brotherhood thing."

"Yes." He tucked his hands behind his back. "After you, *señorita*."

"I've never been on an altar," she said, feeling odd as she stepped forward and passed the low wooden railings that marked the priest's area. It somehow did feel more holy, and the altar itself was so insistently drawing her forward that she had no time to think about just how odd she felt. Her palms practically burned to feel it, and she reached out with both hands and pressed them to the wood, as if her flesh was putty and she was imprinting the designs.

And in a way, she was. Her strongest method of gathering information had always been touch, and she remembered more when her hands were involved. This wood was cool, thickly painted, well tended, and yet, below it all, she could sense the artist who had created it, could almost see him out of the corner of her eye, his tools in hand, his robes long around his legs.

James said, quietly behind her, "What do you feel?"

She closed her eyes. "Love."

Perhaps it was the priest in him, but he seemed to understand she needed to be quiet, to feel things. He waited quietly nearby without fidgeting or rustling. Just waiting.

After a few minutes, she realized she could feel him as strongly as she felt the spirit of the altar. His body, a foot or two away, pulled at her. She could smell the shampoo in his hair, and more. The scent of him, wafting around her. "I don't mind if you feel it, too," she said.

"No?" He stepped next to her, and put his hands on the wood, too. "What am I trying to feel?"

"Whatever," she said. "There are no rules."

His hands were lean and graceful, a warm cinnamon next to her carp-white flesh. His forearm was corded, his wrist strong. It just touched her own. Electric.

She looked up at him, and he was gazing down at her, just so steadily, so clearly. She felt captured, aroused, dizzy—

Abruptly she dropped her hands and moved away. "This is weird. I need some air."

"Wait," James said. "Let's talk a minute in here first. Where no one will overhear us."

She stepped off the dais and turned around. "All right."

James still stood on the platform, and for one swift moment, she saw him as he might have been as a priest, that sensual mouth and haunted face framed by the white collar, his hair trimmed neatly. Why had he turned away from the call?

"When you stand up there," she asked boldly, perhaps hoping to push him away a little, "do you wish you'd stayed in seminary?"

He paused, looked around him, shook his head slowly. "It was not this I wanted, exactly, sermons and the Eucharist."

She plopped down on the first pew. "What did you want?"

"A story for another day," he said, and stepped down

and joined her on the pew. "We must find Claude's story for now, and hope it shows up who wanted him dead."

"Agreed." She lifted a shoulder. "I didn't find out much, honestly. Christie really loved Claude, that's all. Oh, and Christie also lived in Bavaria at one time. Why did that ring a bell?"

"That's where the art dealer is from. Franz?"

"Oh, yeah! Renate Franz. She has a gallery in New York, and she was selling Claude's paintings by the zillions, for very good prices."

"She has a gallery here, too."

Miranda's eyebrows flew upward. "Really?"

"Maybe you should meander down there and see if she's around, or when she's been here. What her alibi might have been."

"You think she would kill an artist to make the prices go up?"

"Not without a little more sweetening in the pot." He tugged a small notebook out of his front pocket and made a note. "Maybe they had an affair."

"I think Tam might have suspected they did. I'll talk to him, too."

"Maybe I'll talk to Tam—man to man, you know— and you see what you can find out about Renate." He stood. "Do you mind being an extra pair of hands? We can get it done more quickly."

"I don't mind." She stood up, too. "You can tell me about the casino as we walk back to the pub, and there you can buy me some lunch for my trouble."

He chuckled. "It's a deal."

Miranda turned to head toward the door, and suddenly James grabbed her sleeve, tugged her back, nudging her shoulder around. Very quietly, he said, "Look."

A pillar of milky sunlight arrowed through one of the high windows and fell on the altar, illuminating the face of the Madonna perfectly—her tiny smile, her outstretched hands, and a dancing halo of black and cobalt butterflies. The small hairs on Miranda's body rose, and she shivered.

James stepped very close to her, the heat of his body radiating over the entire length of hers. A hand fell on her shoulder, pushed away the thick hair and touched the bare skin at her shoulder. His voice murmured into her ear. "Do you think She is giving us a sign?"

"What kind of sign?"

"I don't know." His fingers moved tantalizingly up her nape, brushed her earlobe, her jaw. "To believe."

She didn't want to move. Her skin vibrated where he touched her, and his breath swept her cheek. "In what?"

"Ourselves, perhaps." His fingers threaded gently through her hair. His body moved infinitesimally closer until they were just barely touching. His other hand curled around her waist. "In this." He leaned in close and touched his nose to her ear. In a hushed, nearly inaudible voice, he murmured, "I have never wanted to touch a woman in so many ways as you make me think of. I know you feel it, too."

"Yes," she whispered, leaning backward so her head nested against his shoulder, a small release. A relief.

His fingers floated up the length of her throat, arousing her flesh millimeter by millimeter, and when he took her earlobe in his mouth, she gasped softly.

A door swung open behind them and they broke apart guiltily. The light prevented them from seeing who entered, but flustered, they clasped hands and dashed toward the door anyway, giggling like middle schoolers.

The woman coming in froze, her body stiff and disapproving as she stared at them. At first, Miranda thought it was an old woman, and ducked her head in deference, cloaking herself in youth and zest. It was only as they were about to pass that Miranda saw the woman's feet, clad in blue deck shoes, and she looked up to see Christie Lundgren.

Miranda slowed, meeting the girl's eye, wanting to find a way to reach out to her, to find a way they could all work together. But just as Miranda would have reached for the girl's hand, Christie reeled back, as if in revulsion.

Shocked, Miranda didn't move immediately, not until James nudged her between her shoulder blades. "Never mind," he said, and took her hand again, into the dazzling day.

James tugged her around the side of a tree and into an alley where the heat of the day had built into a cocoon against the stone church, and with little grace, he pushed her against the hot wall, clasped her face in his hands and kissed her.

Heat pushed through her clothes from the wall, melting her buttocks, her shoulder blades, the back of her head. Heat from his body burned against her breasts, her belly, her thighs.

And all of it was forgotten in the taste of his mouth, not a simple tasting kind of kiss, but a fierce, plundering dive to which she opened with alarming and irresistible hunger. His tongue plunged deep, and she met it with a thrust of her own, their lips bruising against teeth.

She had no idea how long it lasted, how long she tossed on that wave of sensuality. Long enough that her breasts felt heavy, and her hips softened and she had to cling to his shoulders to stand upright. He tasted of denial and longings only hinted at and of knowledge of a woman.

At last he raised his head and Miranda opened her eyes to look up at him. His dark eyes boiled with unspoken things, with curiosity and sex and regret. His thumb traced her cheekbone, her jaw.

"Now what do we do?" she said.

"I don't know. Eat?"

"Ah. Yes, let's do."

But even as they turned toward the street, Miranda's cell phone rang with the song that meant Juliet was calling, the *Dragnet* theme song.

Miranda frowned. "Wonder what's going on *now?*" She flipped the phone open. "Please tell me that our parents have not arrived early."

"No. It's bad news, though. Desi was hit by a car. She's at the emergency room."

Chapter 7

At the Mariposa County Hospital, Juliet was waiting for Miranda. James had come with her, and he settled on a white chair in the waiting room. "You go. I'll be here."

She squeezed his hand and rushed with Juliet to an examining room. Desi, wrapped in a blanket, sat on the end of a bed, her arm connected to a saline drip. She leaned dully against Tam's chest. He looked thunderous.

"Oh, Desi!" Juliet cried and rushed forward. "Oh, honey!"

Miranda held back. Desi's face was smeared with red earth, and a scrape marred her forehead, and she had a fat lip. By the way she held her upper body, it was plain there was more.

Juliet examined Desi closely, her hands fluttering over her older sister's head, shoulders, not actually touching her, but waving her hands over the air around Desi. Miranda wanted to ask, but was afraid to—

Juliet asked it all. "What happened? Where are you hurt?" She took a breath, touched her own diaphragm. "Is the baby okay?"

Desi's eyes welled with a vast wash of tears, but she nodded. "They're going to keep me overnight, but it seems to be fine. I'm fat enough to cradle the uterus."

"Desi!"

Tam said, rubbing her back in a slow circle, "It's actually true. Her cushioning cradled the baby."

"I have a bruise on my hip, but I took the brunt of the landing on my shoulder."

"Is something broken?" Miranda asked, noting again the awkward angle at which Desi sat.

"My arm and collarbone."

Miranda let out a breath. "Do you have to go to bed for a few days?"

Desi nodded. Tam stroked her hair, her back. "I'll stay with Tam, so he can check on me and wait on me hand and foot. The dogs will need a place to go."

"Don't worry about it right now," Juliet said.

Miranda, unable to bear being so far apart, moved closer and put her hand on Desi's hair. "I'm glad you're okay."

Desi touched her hand. "It's okay, honey."

"I'm not five, you know," she said with a smile. And was secretly glad that Desi still babied her. In a dry voice she said, "This is just a ploy to get away from the incoming parents, isn't it?"

Juliet chuckled. "Yeah, thanks a lot, girl."

"What am I going to do for the wedding?" Desi said, suddenly, her eyes wide with panic. "I'm going to have my arm in a sling and a cast up to *here!*"

"Ha!" Miranda felt like a hero. "As it happens, I have a guy from Denver bringing some saris to town. He'll be here tomorrow with a bunch for you to choose from."

"I don't know how to wear a sari!"

"I'll help you," Miranda said. "One of my friends wears them a lot for various family things."

"You'll look beautiful," Tam said. "It'll suit you."

"The wedding is not the most important thing here, guys," Juliet broke in. "What the hell happened?"

"I was crossing the street by the clinic and some-body knocked me down with a car."

"They didn't stop?"

Desi looked wan. She shook her head.

"Did you see anything, Desi?" Juliet asked, taking her good hand. "Anything at all?"

"Not really. It's not like I wasn't looking where I was going. I had lunch at the pub and walked back toward the clinic. I do it almost every day, and I take the back way so it's not so crowded. I guess I just didn't see the guy."

"Was it a car or a truck?" Juliet asked.

"Car."

"Blue, white, black, yellow?"

Desi looked into the distance. "Not black. Some-thing lighter." She frowned. "I have a sense of it being a little bit older, with one of those big grates, you know?" She sighed. "But don't people remember strange things?"

"Sometimes they remember right, too," Juliet said. "Good work."

"Have the police been here?" Miranda asked.

"They brought her in. Somebody saw her lying on the side of the road." Tam's voice grew rough and he put his nose against Desi's hair. He swore softly.

Miranda didn't blame him. She exchanged a look with Juliet. "James is waiting out there. We're going to go talk to some people this afternoon." She eased close and patted Desi's leg. "I'll be back tonight, sis."

"You don't have to, Mirrie."

Stung, Miranda met her sister's eyes. "I need to know you're all right. Can I take care of the dogs or something? Something practical?"

"That would actually be very helpful. Josh can drive you up if you're uncomfortable driving my truck."

"I'll take care of it." She headed back out to the waiting room, her heart pounding furiously. James stood when he saw her, his face grave.

"Is she all right?"

"Barely. Some idiot nearly killed her with a car and just kept driving."

James's eyes narrowed. "Did the police think it was an accident?"

"I don't know."

"Let's go get some food and then chat up some people who might know something."

* * *

Bill Biloxi was a developer who owned several hundred acres adjoining Desi's, and his wife was the elegantly beautiful Elsa Franz. James figured the pair of them were a good place to start. After a quick lunch from a sandwich shop, he and Miranda drove up the narrow, twisting road through thick forests of ponderosa and lodge pole pines, and stands of aspens shaking their silvery-green leaves in the bright day. It was impossible not to admire it. "Hard to imagine anything more gorgeous than this," he commented, his hands loose on the steering wheel.

"It's pretty," Miranda agreed. "I used to hate coming up here for camp, but now I can't remember why. After the East Village, it's very peaceful."

"I bet." The curving road suddenly rose to the top of the hill and deposited them at an enormous mansion built in an agreeably tasteful mountain style, gray flagstone and thick timbers. James whistled. "No money there, huh?"

Miranda rolled her eyes. "Who needs ten thousand square feet of house on top of a mountain?"

Mildly he said, "I'm sure they have to do a lot of entertaining."

The front door swung open before they reached it, and a tall, leggy blonde stood there. She wore a crisp, short khaki skirt and a blue halter top that showed off her burnished shoulders and spectacular chest. "Good morning!" she called. "Can I help you?"

The accent was German, or something of that ilk.

"Good morning," James said, smiling at her. Women like this wanted to be admired, and woe be unto you if you didn't pay homage.

She smiled back, politely.

James extended his hand, waiting to speak until they were face-to-face, eye to eye. There was a faint reserve about her, but it felt normal. "I'm James Marquez," he said. "I was hoping to be able to talk to you about Claude Tsosie."

He'd taken her hand for a reason. She yanked out of his grip, but couldn't exactly slam the door in his face. "No," she said. "I've said all that I want to say."

Miranda came forward, a beauty in her own right, and he saw Elsa notice. "If you won't talk to him, maybe you'll talk to me. I'm Desi Rousseau's sister. She's a good woman, and you know it."

A flicker over the aquamarine eyes, a faint, acknowledging tilt of the elegant jaw. "Tam is my friend."

"If we can't crack this case, Desi's going to end up in jail," Miranda said.

"If she lives that long," James added. "She was run down by a car this morning."

"Oh my God!" Her eyes widened. "Was she hurt?"

"Her collarbone is broken," Miranda said harshly. "And were you aware that she's carrying a child? *Tam's* child?"

"No! I—"

From within, a male voice said, "Who is it, Elsa?"

She threw an alarmed glance over her shoulder and called out, "I'll be there in a minute, baby." Furtively she pulled the heavy door mostly closed and stepped onto the porch. "My husband does not want me to talk about this."

"Why?"

She shrugged. "He's angry, yes? There is a big land deal he wanted to make and it didn't go through."

James remembered the article in the newspaper, and made a mental note to go back through and read it again. "It's not just any deal, though, is it?" he said, partly to Miranda, partly to Elsa, "There's an enclosed aquifer below Desi's property that could be worth billions, isn't that right?"

Elsa waved a hand. "A lot of money. I don't know about that part."

"What about Claude?"

"A lot of people were mad at him."

"You?"

She shook her head, mouth turning at the corners. "Not me."

Miranda said, "He wasn't your type was he?"

The blonde's nostrils flared slightly. Derision? Amusement? James couldn't tell. "No."

"Are you related to Renate Franz?" Miranda asked.

Elsa's head jerked around. For one long moment, she stared at Miranda. "It is no secret," she said, though it obviously had not occurred to many. "She is my sister."

The door behind her jerked open and Bill Biloxi, a handsome, fit man well into his fifties, glowered out at them. "What do you want?"

"Just talking," James said.

"They're just going," Elsa said, giving them a hard look.

"Yes," James said, taking Miranda's arm firmly. She looked volatile. Fierce. "Thanks for your time."

As they walked away, Miranda flung her arm out of his hand. "Why don't we talk to *him?* He probably knows all kinds of things."

"I'm sure he does. But he's not going to tell us and it will only antagonize his wife. She knows something, too."

"Do you think so?"

He glanced back at the gabled house. "Oh, yeah." He opened the door to the car. "Let's go check your sister's dogs, and then I want you to call Renate's gallery."

Miranda nodded. Her mouth, that luscious, rich, kissable mouth, was sulky, but she climbed in the car without saying anything else.

Once settled, she slumped in the seat and rubbed her forehead. "We've gotta get to the bottom of this, James," she said in a hoarse voice. "My sister really doesn't deserve this. She's honestly one of the best human beings I've ever known, and she hasn't had that much happiness in her life."

He touched her hand. "We will." He thought of the notes in his hotel room and the interviews yet to do. "Let's just get the dogs fed and make sure everything is all right there, then I'm going to drop you off and let you make some phone calls."

She nodded. For a long while they were quiet, and between them lay that kiss, so hot and wet and full of promises he probably shouldn't make. Bad idea to get mixed up with a client, even worse with one who was so plainly out of his league, and nursing a broken heart and as hungry for positive attention as a fatherless fourteen-year-old. A twist moved in his gut.

"Then what?" she asked into the silence.

"I'm turning in early," he said. "I've got a race in three days."

"Ah." She sank down lower in her seat. "Turn at the next right."

Guilt moved through his lungs. "Miranda, I think—"

She flipped her hair over one shoulder to pin him with her fierce blue gaze. "Don't, okay? I'm tired of everyone patronizing me. I'm sure you have lots of good reasons, but you can keep them."

Over the glaze of reddish yearning he felt for her, he saw a face that still haunted him. A face that revealed his weakness, his unbridled lack of control over his emotions. "I'm not who you think I am, who you want me to be, Miranda."

"I'm sure. Men never are." She took a breath. "I'd rather not talk about this anymore."

"Fair enough," he said, and turned up the volume on the radio.

By the time he dropped her off at Juliet's house, Miranda was hungry enough to eat cockroaches raw. She'd had scones this morning and a quick sandwich at lunch. Now, late afternoon, her stomach was growling so loudly she didn't care about anything—not an old boyfriend or one she sort of wanted or her sister in the hospital or anything except *food*. In the fridge, there was little to choose from. A bottle of milk, a grim bit of butter, not much else. She took the strawberries from the shelf and started devouring them as she looked for other things. Graham crackers. Soft cubes of some processed cheese thing. Enough for now.

She poured a big glass of water and carried it all out to the backyard. A picnic table with an umbrella stood beneath a tree, looking west to the opening of the canyon.

It really was a remarkable view, she thought, admiring the levels of blues, layer upon layer into the distance, contrasted by soft green falls of long-needled pines and rattling aspens and the clay-red earth.

Which made her think of Desi's dirt-smeared cheek, her wan and fearful expression in the hospital this morning. Had it been an accident or something more sinister? Who could do such a thing?

She ate a strawberry and thought of Max, telling her that he still thought of her. Asking for—what? Absolution? Attention?

And as she broke a graham cracker in half, she thought of James's fingers drifting over her throat inside the church, thought of the dash into the alley, the press of his body against hers, the thrust of his tongue in her mouth, so expert.

With a soft moan, she bent her head to the table. What a day!

From within the house came a clatter, and Juliet's voice called, "Hello?"

"Backyard," Miranda called back.

Juliet came through, wisps of hair falling out of her ponytail in just the right way. Her cheeks were flushed. "It's hot!" she said, popping open a can of soda.

"How's Desi?" Juliet asked. "I had an emergency and didn't get back to the hospital this afternoon."

"She's okay. Broken wrist, broken clavicle, bumps and bruises, but the baby seems absolutely fine. They're keeping her tonight, and I guess she'll stay with Tam for a day or two. Josh picked up the dogs, so don't worry about that." She took a long swallow of root beer.

"How did your day go? Find anything? Solve the murder for all time?"

"Not yet. I've got to make some phone calls in a few minutes, but I was starving. There is no real food in this house, in case you haven't noticed."

"Probably won't be for a few days, either. I ate with Josh and Glory. We have too much going on and we'll be eating out or with our parents."

Memory slammed her and she jerked her head up. "Our parents are going to be here tomorrow, aren't they?"

Juliet took a breath, blew it out. "Sadly, yes. They're staying at the hotel."

"All the better to avoid them."

"Right. Well, maybe it won't be so bad. They're getting older now, you know. Mom just turned sixty-nine. How much trouble can two old people be?"

Miranda just looked at her. "My mother," she said succinctly, "will never be an old person."

Juliet chuckled. "True. But it's my wedding. You

can't blame me for hoping." Tugging the scrunchie from her hair, she said with an arched brow, "So… James. A little chemistry there, huh?"

"No," Miranda said, as if her sister had lost her marbles.

Juliet snorted. "Right."

"There isn't. Or if there is, I'm not going to let it go anywhere."

"You've got to let your guard down sometimes, sister dear."

"See, there's where you're wrong. No, I don't."

Juliet nodded, her mouth tipped in a tiny smile. "That's what I thought, too."

"I'm pretty sure there's nothing more annoying than a woman smugly in love with one of the last five good guys on the planet."

"Touché." Laughing, Juliet stood. "I'm going to take a shower, let you make your phone calls."

Miranda shrugged. But as Juliet left her, she wondered what was going on in James's mind, to make him come on to her, then put up walls to keep her out. She fingered her cell phone, brought up the outgoing calls list and saw the Hotel Mariposa on there. What if she just called and asked? Reasonably. Maturely.

Nice trick, that.

And yet, she was tired of wishy-washy men. Seeing how Tam looked at Desi, and the way Josh lit up when Juliet came in a room made her want the real thing for herself. This business of hot and cold, up and down, madly in love, then…not. Forget it.

The number she did dial was for her friend Alexis, a fellow artist who would know the numbers Miranda needed in the art community. She planned to talk with Renate under the guise of being an artist seeking a gallery, but she also wanted to call other galleries, see what the art community had to say about the Bavarian dealer and her famous dead client.

Back in his hotel room, James lay flat on the bed with the idea of a nap. His body eased into the mattress, and he mentally ran over his body, checking for sore or tight spots. A little weariness on the back of his left hamstring, up into the glute. Running uphill, he tended to lead a little hard with his left foot. His shoulders were tight. Low in his groin was thick tension.

Not from running, at least physically. He was adamantly running away from Miranda Rousseau and her blasted lace bras and Botticelli hair and quivering lush lips. The taste of her lingered in his imagination—hints of chocolate and spice and the long heat of a summer afternoon. It was all too easy to imagine her long white body stripped of all its protective layers, beneath his in this very bed. Her skin would be delicately white, run through with bluish veins, her pubic hair as red and startling as her hair.

With a groan, he rolled over on his belly. Enough.

He hadn't been smitten by a woman in a long time, not since Rita Valdez when he was twenty-one, and his ego and self-esteem were freshly bruised by his recognition that he did not have the temperament to be a good priest. He'd gone to the police academy instead, and Rita had sauntered into class that first morning, all siren curves she tried to contain and could not, her long, dark eyes and red lips an invitation she tried not to issue.

They were from the same general area, the high, secluded mountains of northern New Mexico, and she had as many bruises as he did—her heart had been broken by an early divorce, and she'd come to Albuquerque to get away from the reminders of how she'd failed to do the one thing that was expected of her.

He resisted her until the end of their academy training, then asked her to dinner and she invited him back to her apartment, where he, at long last, sated his insane lust for her in a session that lasted what felt like days. He could not get enough of her—her beautiful curves, her laughing mouth, her long hair tangling on the pillow. When she was dressed and he saw the upper curve of a breast, he would think with satisfaction that he'd tasted that entire slope.

She'd broken his heart, but only in the way that a first love always breaks a heart. They grew apart and Rita was smart enough to know it wasn't going to last so she broke it off. Cleanly, with great compassion, so that they didn't have to hurt each other by one or the other falling in love with someone else. He'd moped for months, but in the end, he had found other women attractive.

Not like this. Not this instant, furious, almost irresistible attraction. Everything in him was drawn to her, as if she were a magnet and he needed to touch every cell in her with every cell in him.

And vice versa. He knew she was feeling the same thing, the inexplicable need to meld. He'd tasted it in her kiss, felt it in the way she pressed upward into him, her hands restlessly pulling at his shirt, weaving over his shoulders and hair.

Troubling him was the gulf between them in terms of class. She had traveled widely, been all over the world, lived in New York City. She was an artist, a successful one, and he was a private eye. She was white, raised by East Coast bohemians. He was Latin, raised by a ranch hand and a housewife in a cottage where he slept in a room with three of his brothers.

In some ways, he was the superior, perhaps. He could think more clearly. He had faith and she had none. He had steadiness of purpose and dedication and athleticism.

Perhaps what he offered was a balance for what she gave.

It felt important, this meeting with this woman, as if many things had had to be arranged in order for them to meet. A song wound through his head, a line about seeing his children in her eyes.

Madre! It didn't have to be such a big drama. He rolled over and picked up the phone.

Two hours later, the information was compelling enough that Miranda thought maybe she *should* call James, just to let him know what was going on.

As she was considering it, the phone rang in her

hand. She saw the hotel number and tossed her head, putting as much coolness in her voice as possible. "Hello?"

"Hello, Miranda," James said in his softly accented voice. "I called to apologize. I have a story I would like to tell you if you wouldn't mind."

"I already told you we don't have to do this."

"Perhaps that's true," he said agreeably, "but it appears that my brain will not stop giving me visions of that kiss we shared this afternoon. It was rare and good. Will you give me a second chance?"

All at once, Miranda was furious. "No," she said.

A thick, long silence at the other end of the line. Then, "Very well. My apologies."

Coolly, she said, "I made some phone calls this afternoon, as you asked, and I'll be happy to meet with you in the morning if you like."

A soft pause. "All right. At ReNew, then? Eight o'clock?"

"Yes. That will be fine."

"See you then."

Miranda hung up with a sense of virtuously overcoming some dire temptation—Black Forest Cake or a pint of Cherry Garcia. She jumped up and went into the house to find Juliet dozing on the couch, her mouth open softly. Poor thing. She'd been running around like crazy. She left a note on the counter: *Gone to get a sandwich.*

It felt good to get outside and move, Miranda thought. Whenever she came to Mariposa, it was as if she became someone else, a woman who liked to be outside and walk around, who traded in her high heels for walking sandals and delicate silk T-shirts for cotton tanks.

Which was the real woman? Which was the fake? Was she a city girl? Or a mountain mama? Was she the restless wanderer, seeking new friends and new experiences in villages and cities the world over? She didn't know.

Unbidden came a question: What setting would create the best environment for her work?

It startled her enough that she stopped dead in the street and looked up at the mountains around her. At the sky. The colorful humans streaming by. Some little voice inside of her said, we want some peace and quiet.

She scowled. Right. For how long would she like it?

You'd have to be insane not to appreciate this, she thought, coming onto Black Diamond Boulevard. Long, gold light poured through the break in the mountains at the end of the canyon as the sun sank toward the horizon. It was perhaps an hour till sundown, and the entire valley was saturated with a light so astonishing she wanted to bottle it. The artist in her tried to name it—*gold mist, topaz haze, yellow gauze*—but none of them were quite right.

Half the town was out on foot. She nodded and smiled as she passed other amblers, the odd cyclist riding home from the trails, the packs of hikers coming into town after hiking the trails from Ordway, just over the other side of the mountain. The bakery she had in mind was packed with people waiting, so she veered off to her left, walked a couple of blocks over and dipped into the organic grocery store instead. She'd just pick up the makings of a sandwich and take them back home.

Grabbing a chunk of foccacia, she headed down the narrow aisle and turned into the dairy aisle, and there— of course—was James. He didn't see her right away, his head bent over something in his hand. His silky black hair fell forward like water, touching the high cut of cheekbone. He was lean and still, like a wolf, wearing a neatly pressed red cotton shirt tucked into a pair of jeans. Walking sandals that matched her own on his feet. Reading glasses on his nose.

She could have slipped away, forgotten the cheese, left it alone. But he looked so...*good*. On so many levels. Honorable good. Responsible good. Healthy good. Delicious good. Sexy good.

And instead of retreating, she stood her ground, waiting for him to feel her gaze and notice her. When he did, his expression immediately blazed into something happier, and that was good, too. "Hi," he said with a crooked smile. The glasses made him look different, more approachable and interesting.

"Hi." She moved toward him. "There were too many people at the Bread Company, so I came here instead."

He nodded. Pleased. Waiting.

"I guess," Miranda said, "maybe it's a sign."

"Ah." He took his glasses off, met her eyes full-on. "Then perhaps you would have a picnic supper with me and we can tell our stories, hmm?"

A soft red cloud surrounded them, streaked with the gold of hope, and Miranda breathed it in, smelling fresh grass and the vanilla notes of ponderosa pines. "All right. Where do you want to go?"

He smiled. "That is a surprise. Come with me."

Chapter 8

Miranda felt both shy and exhilarated as they wandered through the old-fashioned little grocery store, picking out things for their picnic. Brown-skinned pears and white cheese and the cheesy foccacia bread she'd already chosen. Imported ginger beer in brown bottles, her choice; big pink and green cookies from the bakery section, his choice. Fragrant turkey breast, cut fresh from a bird just taken from the oven, skin crackling brown and shiny. It smelled so heavenly, Miranda's mouth watered.

Neither of them had a pack, but Miranda had brought a canvas bag with her and they loaded everything into it, then James led the way down the street to the trams that ran eighteen hours a day to carry tourists and workers back and forth to the restaurant at the top of the mountain and the bedroom town of Allen, a mainly residential area on the other side of the mountain where the workers in Mariposa could afford to rent apartments.

As they waited for a car, James said, "How is your sister? Any word?"

"She's staying the night in the hospital," Miranda said, and repeated what she'd told Juliet. "I'll go see her in the morning. The sari guy is coming from Denver."

"Hop on," James said as a car rolled up, slowly moving.

She ducked into the car and he settled beside her. It swung a little beneath their weight, then slowly moved up the mountain. "There is someone bringing saris to Mariposa for you to look at?"

"Yes. Desi needs something to wear for the wedding, and I shopped all morning trying to find something. I finally thought a sari would suit her."

"It seems a long way to come to sell saris."

She shrugged. "He'll be paid well for his trouble."

"Ah." He picked up her hand, held it. "Do you mind?"

"No." She folded her fingers around his and admired the expanding view, more spectacular with every foot. The car moved at a leisurely pace up, rising over an aspen grove, thin white arms shaking round leaves in the breeze, and a winding road and areas that would be ski slopes in the winter. A knot of backpackers made their way down a path, their long day almost at an end.

"I've always wondered what it would have been like to travel that way," James said.

"It's great," she said. "Why didn't you?"

His eyes on the hikers, he said, "I grew up in a little town in New Mexico. It would not have occurred to any of us to do something like that. Going to Albuquerque or Pueblo was a big trip, you know." He grinned, teeth white and perfect, as if to belie to his small-town roots.

"So how did you get to Albuquerque? That's where you live now, isn't it?"

"Yes." He gestured to bring her attention to the peaks coming into view over the trees. "My sister's husband joined the Army during the first Gulf War, and they moved to Albuquerque. He, uh, didn't adjust well when he came home, so I went to live with her and her two kids, help out. A man in the house, so to speak."

"How old were you?"

"Seventeen." He raised one side of his mouth. The expression was rakish, charming. "Full of everything but sense."

"Been there," she said.

"Her husband was unreliable, drinking too much and never home, and when he was, he was not really there, you know? His eyes looked inward. He killed himself about six months into my time there, a Gulf War casualty. There have been a lot of them."

"James! I am so sorry!"

James shrugged. "He needed some help he didn't get, to deal with the things he saw. Stinking bodies. Blown-up vehicles. Alice had three little boys. I lived with her, after, taking care of the boys while she worked two jobs." He leaned into her, and pleased in some wordless way, Miranda leaned back. "I learned to cook and clean and give everybody baths."

"Better than I ever did," Miranda said. "There's always been someone to do that for me."

"Such a little princess," he said, and stung, she looked up, but he was smiling.

"I guess I am in a way. So, didn't you hate it, having to do all that when you were a kid?"

"No, I liked it. I had to sleep on the couch, but it was still better than back home, which was too many people all the time, too much noise, and my dad smoking cigarettes all the time. I mean, I don't blame him. Everybody smoked up there and he was a hardworking man without many pleasures, but I hated it."

"Did you always run?"

He nodded. "Long as I can remember. One of the teachers in my middle school was a marathoner, and I thought it was incredible that somebody could run that way. I found out I had some talent."

Miranda grinned. "*Some* talent?"

"A little." He looked at her. "You're teasing me."

"A little," she echoed. So close, she could see the places along his chin where his beard would come in. A freckle by his eye. The tiniest threading of pale gold through his dark irises. She knew she should look at the view, but looking at James was better.

"Look!" he cried, and pointed at a hawk sailing below them.

She laughed in purest delight. Higher in the air than a hawk. Imagine!

They sat there like that, holding hands, looking at the view, the only sound the motors pulling the tram up the hill. At one point, it stopped, the car swinging gently high above a slope carpeted with thick green grass and wildflowers. "What happened?"

"Sometimes they just stop it for a minute to get something on a car, or help somebody off. Who knows?"

"Not a bad place to spend a few minutes," she said. "Quite a view."

"Yes, there is," he said and touched her cheek.

"Sweet talker."

In a moment, they started moving again, and in another moment, the car bumped into the housing where a boy opened the door for them. Miranda and James jumped out.

He gestured for her to follow and they headed uphill, past the restaurant and the ski patrol. Miranda had to stop and catch her breath after only a few feet. "Wait! I can't breathe."

"Sorry!" He peered at her face. "Are you light-headed? Headachy?"

"Light-headed. A little dizzy."

He smiled gently. "We're at about twelve thousand feet or better. Not a lot of oxygen up here."

"It feels funny."

"We're just going to that group of trees right there. Do you see them?"

Miranda breathed in through her nose slowly,

feeling better. The trees were about a few hundred feet away, up a gradual slope. "Yes. I can do that."

"We'll just go very slowly. Don't talk." He took the bag she had slung over her shoulder. "Once we're sitting down, it should be okay, and we're going down on the way back."

She nodded. It took all of her concentration to put one foot in front of the other, and she had to stop twice on the hill to catch her breath. "Damn," she exclaimed the second time. "I feel like an old lady!" Sweat popped up along her neck and she raised a heavy arm to her hair, pulling it over her shoulder.

"You're doing great, actually." He gave her a bottle of water. "Have a big sip. It's easy to get dehydrated up here, too."

Miranda breathed, drank, handed him back the bottle and started trudging toward their destination.

At last, they made it to the trees. A wide, flat rock sat on the hill, a perfect granite table, and Miranda collapsed on it. "Finally!" With a not-entirely-fake gasp, she fell backward and closed her eyes, breathing in the fine, oxygen-depleted air. It felt lighter than any air she'd ever experienced, but she also felt a bit like she was underwater. Her senses felt a little watery.

"Are you okay?" James asked.

She opened one eye. "Is this a test? Because I think I'm flunking."

"Not at all." He gave her a pear. "Sit up and look at your reward."

Miranda flung an arm over her eyes. "It's the moun-

tains. It's Mariposa," she said. "It's always spectacular. One *Sound of Music* view after another."

He laughed. "Was I right about the altar?" He
nudged her. "Sit up."

"You were, sir." She hauled herself upright. And
looked.

And blinked.

"Wow." The rock sat on a small mesa, surrounded
on all sides by the harsh, craggy peaks of the San Juans,
all at an altitude of thirteen thousand to fourteen thousand feet. The Mariposa valley divided them neatly, and
far, far below twinkled the first streetlights in the dusky
shadows. It looked like a toy railroad town, with plastic
broccoli trees and traffic lights changing from green to
red and teeny, tiny neon signs. From this vantage point,
she could also see Allen on the other side of the mountain, far more spreading, with bigger parking lots and
open fields and parks.

But the most spectacular thing was the sun, which
hung like a molten gold ball to the west. Long, long bars
of light arrowed into canyons and misted over certain
streets and cast shadows of boulders three thousand feet
below.

She grinned at James. "Okay, so it's better views
than *The Sound of Music.*"

A low, earthy chuckle escaped him and he started
putting their supper out on the sparkly gray rock.

"You actually run up here, don't you?" she asked
suddenly.

"I do." The words were not the least apologetic. He

bit cleanly into a pear, chewed meditatively. "It's like nothing else."

"I keep wondering how my father is going to do this race. I mean, he's old—like seventy-five. Who does a long run like this when they're seventy-five?"

"Lotta people. Some tough old birds out there. Is your dad like that?"

Miranda almost snorted, but a sudden vision of her father coming down a mountain in Zurich, sweaty and pleased, flashed in memory. "He's always liked running, and I think he specifically likes mountain running. He did it a lot it Europe."

"The race is Saturday. When will he be here?"

"Tomorrow," she said with the inevitable sigh. "They're coming from the house in the French Alps, so I'm sure he's been training along with drinking his martinis."

James grinned. "It's good to see a woman who is so devoted to her parents."

"I haven't heard you talk about yours."

"My father passed about three years ago. My mother is—she just is a woman of her times and her place."

Miranda started to feel better, more acclimatized. She broke off a chunk of bread and spread soft cheese on it. "Is she part of the story you were going to tell me?"

The brightness bled from his face. "No."

"I'm sorry," Miranda said. "Don't go there if you don't want to. I apologize."

"It's all right." He broke a piece of cookie off the

main body and ate it. "You asked why I did not become a priest. People generally assume it was a woman. It was, but not in the way most people think."

Miranda tightened her hand. "James, let's not talk about anything dark or sad or in the past, all right? We have this beautiful view, and this good food, and—" She took a breath. "I guess I'm just tired of thinking about what once was, instead of what is."

For a long moment, he looked at her, his beautiful mouth sober. Then he leaned in and kissed her, very gently. "Thank you."

The tenderness in his lips made her heart catch. Bending her head, she focused on the food. "Now, tell me how you became a private detective. I think I remember reading on the Web site that you were a cop."

"I was," he said. "It's a simple story. I felt I could do more good working independently. Often, a difficult case requires more time than can be afforded by the police."

"That makes sense."

"It occurs to me, Miranda, that you are a very good listener. I have told you my stories and you have not told me yours."

"You haven't told me why you gave up the seminary."

His eyes darkened dangerously. "We're leaving it in the past, remember?"

"Yes. You're right." Twisting the stem from a pear, she shrugged. "I don't have very good stories."

"Oh, come on. How did you become an artist?"

"I think I always was one. I clearly remember the first time I discovered felt—color you could hold in your hands. It was just so thrilling, being able to handle it and cut it and glue it. I made a bunch of little wall hangings for my sisters and I." She grinned, remembering the bead-crusted works. "They were so good to me, those two."

"Did you go to art school?"

"I did. And studied in Europe, and I got lucky, met some of the right people and got into a good gallery where the mass marketers found me. So I can have money and be an artist, which is sort of rare." She swallowed pear and raised a finger. "Which makes me think of Claude, who is a highly valued commodity now that he's dead, and the phone calls I made this afternoon."

"I'm all ears."

She sucked in a gulping measure of air. "I had to breathe."

"I understand."

"I wasn't able to talk with Renate Franz. They said she's out of town, so we'll have to reach her later, but I did talk to some other people I know, some gallery owners and members of the art community in New York, and it was kind of interesting." A soft breeze blew strands of hair over her face, and Miranda caught it back with one hand. "It seems Claude was somewhat known around Renate's gallery, that they've been hanging out together for a long, long time."

"She's represented him for a long time, right?"

"No, he didn't start painting until he and Desi moved here to Mariposa."

His eyes narrowed. "Really."

"That it's only been a few years, and suddenly he's that brilliant? I mean, it happens sometimes, but not that often."

"So what's the feeling among the people in your world? That he's a fake?"

Miranda's mouth dropped. "No, actually, but that's brilliant, James. What if he was just being a front man, an ethnic front man, for another painter?"

"And maybe that painter got tired of it."

Miranda grinned. "Painted himself into a corner, though, huh?"

He laughed. "That was terrible."

"Yeah, I know. And we didn't really need another motive for someone to kill Claude. It's like the *Orient Express,* where everyone had reason to kill him."

"Maybe it is something like that, a bunch of people who got together and decided to get rid of him once and for all—ex-lovers, cuckolded husbands, business partners he double-crossed. Everybody."

"Did you just say cuckolded?"

"I did."

"Wow." She fanned herself with exaggerated movements. "I can't resist a man with a great vocabulary!"

The sun made a sudden slip, and the entire world blazed, as if someone in the heavens switched a floodlight marked Pink. Miranda snapped to attention, captured by scarves of pink clouds drifting over the pointed breasts of the mountains, by the trailers of pale gold necklaces draped over the swells and curves.

"Ta da!" James said, spreading his palms. "The artist's palette, spread out just for you."

Dazzled nearly to tears, Miranda opened her eyes wider, as if to take in more of the show. Pale gold and pink melded and the colors of the mountains turned dark blue, and then, as if the heavens were igniting, red flickered from cloud to peak to cloud. Miranda put her hands to her face. Tears leaked from the corner of her eyes, and she blinked them away, embarrassed. "It's amazing!"

He, too, gazed at the sky, his profile almost Mayan. For a moment, Miranda was snared as much by the beauty in his face as by the sky bowled over their heads. His hands rested loosely on his knees, and there was a depth of utter peace and calm about him that drew her like a hearth. It seemed a weary person could rest there, in the pool of quiet, let go of the tangles of tension and spiky drama in her chest.

A small voice in her head murmured, *uh, oh—better be careful with this one.*

She ignored it, leaned into him, her arm touching his arm, her cheek against the red cotton of his shirt. "Thank you, again."

"My pleasure." He touched her nose, brushed her chin with one finger, as if surprised by the shape, as if he'd never seen nose or chin before. For a single moment, he looked down at her, and their eyes met, a single moment that felt to Miranda as if the rest of everything hung in the balance.

Here, now.

"There is a Navajo chant that says, *You see I stand*

in good relation to you...I am alive, I am alive," he said
quietly, his finger now brushing the angle of her cheekbone. "In this moment, I am alive."

The vivid pink light edged his hair, cast his tawny
skin in a new light. She could see what he'd looked like
as a boy, and conversely, what he would look like as an
old man, and her heart squeezed so hard she put a hand
to her chest.

Then he bent to kiss her, and they tumbled backward, gently rolling together on the wide flat rock,
laughing as they squashed the remainder of the bread.

He settled nearly on top of her. Miranda welcomed it,
feeling dizzily suspended, as if they were part of the
sunset. He stroked her hair, her cheek, kissed her lightly
and then more deeply. She raised her hands to his hair,
thick and cool and slippery, and touched his ears, his
neck.

And there they were, drifting, melding, alive in the
light, in the airy softness of dusk, lips and hands and
bodies doing the communicating.

"Sorry to break things up, folks," said a voice above
them, "but it's going to be dark as sin in a few minutes
and you need to get on up here."

They broke apart to grin at the man standing on the
road. A man of fifty or so, with a ski patrol jacket and
bushy eyebrows, clapped his hands. "C'mon. Move it."

"No problem," James said, leaping to his feet. He
held out a hand for Miranda, who brushed her hair
down, smoothed her blouse, color burning in her
cheeks.

Chapter 9

They walked back down to the tram station, holding hands in the lavender gloaming and stood in the building waiting for a car. The unfinished kiss was a siren that stretched between them wantonly, and James tried to shake it off. But he felt heat in the oval hollow between their clasped palms, and stroked the delicate skin of her wrist with his thumb. She looked up at him, her eyes both trusting and afraid. He raised her hand to his lips, kissed her knuckles.

A faint smile turned the corners of her red mouth, and she looked away. Shook her head and he was sure it was at herself. "Hey," he said. "It's not imaginary."

For a moment she held his gaze, then looked toward the arriving car. "Here's our ride."

They settled inside, side by side. James moved close, slid an arm around her shoulders. Her hair brushed his arm, light and soft as fur. Amused by the thought, he picked up a lock and rubbed it between his fingers, wondering what kind of animal she would be. Something rare and skittish. A red fox, shy and soft, given beauty by her pelt. He smiled to himself, and at that moment, she looked up again.

Their eyes caught. The only sound was their breath and the machinery moving the car down the mountain in a smooth, easy ride. James admired her mouth, her long eyelashes, her body next to his. Everything about her was soft, so inviting. He bent to kiss her lightly.

She raised her head infinitesimally and pressed her mouth to his, and raised a hand to his jaw, a light, exploratory touch that traced his cheekbone, jawline, the edge of his eye.

He closed his eyes and drank of her mouth, taking his time, easily and without urgency kissing and kissing her, sliding his lips one way, then the other, taking a moment to gauge the lower lip, then lightly touching her upper with his tongue. They kissed all the way down, making out like teenagers, and it felt like each kiss shifted the universe, that each binding moment meant something finer was coming into the world. He felt lost in her, delighted and lost and bemused and breathless.

About halfway down, the car stopped dead, and they broke apart to look at the soft lavender world around them, the scattering of the town below, pristine and perfect. "Wow," Miranda said. "I've had some pretty great dinner dates in my time, but this takes the cake."

"Yeah?" He cupped her cheek, his heart pounding as if he were already in love. "I don't want to seem like a weirdo, but this feels like something rare."

"If you're weird, I am, too." She swallowed.

He kissed her again, drinking deep. They were both dizzy and flushed as they jumped off the tram, and holding hands, dashed like children into the street. "I'll buy you a drink," he said, reluctant to leave her.

"You won't have even one?"

"Not with a race coming up."

"I can respect that," she said. "Sure, I'd love a drink. Let's not go to The Black Crown, though—I'd rather not run into my family or Tam. I doubt any of them are there, but just in case."

"Ashamed of me?" he said lightly.

Her head jerked up. "No! Why would I be?"

Which was more vehement a reaction than he'd expected. "I was only teasing you a little," he said. Slightly troubling, but he brushed it away. *Don't be too sensitive.* Sometimes, pride got in his way. Too much pride.

"Sorry," she said, and pursed her lips. "I know where we'll go. It's only a block or two. I haven't been there before, but I've heard about it. Now I have the perfect reason to try it out."

"Lead on, my lady," he said, and she laughed. They held hands in the mild summer night, joined for a few minutes by a pair of dogs, a blue heeler mix and some sort of spaniel. He was about to worry about them crossing the busy main street, but as if they, too, knew to avoid it, they turned off before they got there. "I worry about dogs too much," he said. "I want them to stay home in their yards, safe and happy."

"Me, too. It makes me crazy that so many of them wander around here. They must get hurt."

"Do you have one?"

"No, I live in a tiny apartment. There's no room for a dog. I thought about getting a cat recently, but honestly, I'm on the road so much that it's just too hard." She stopped in front of a tiny bar with a window painted in blue and red paisleys. Written in sixties rock poster script was The Poppy Seed. "Here we are. Put on your sunglasses, man, and let's go inside."

Inside he chuckled. India cotton tapestries hung on the old walls, probably hiding cracked plaster, and there were soft purple lights glowing at intervals through the room, making square velvet and fluorescent posters glow. "Are those black lights?"

Miranda grinned. "Isn't this the coolest little spot? The jukebox has nothing but a bunch of baby boomer oldies, too—Rolling Stones and The Who and stuff like that."

Customers were a mix of twenty-something backpacker types, tanned and a little grimy, or real ex-hippies and bikers, men and women. The bartender, a man of about sixty with a round tummy like Santa Claus and a beard to match, nodded at them. "I'll have a margarita, please," Miranda said.

The old guy shook his head. "Sorry, sweetheart," he

said in a voice like five miles of mountain road, "we don't do anything that fancy here. Beer and wine, or a whiskey and Coke. I can set up a shot of tequila for you if you want."

Miranda laughed. "No, thanks. How about beer, then?"

"Coke for me," James said.

"Jack and Coke?" He narrowed his eyes. "No, I reckon not. You're a runner, aren't you?"

"I am."

"I used to be," the bartender said, his voice gravelly. "You know Peter Bok lives here."

"I met him! My first day here," James said. "What a guy."

"He comes in here, now and then. His wife likes my French fries, and as long as I've been here, he has a beer a day, at suppertime."

"No kidding." James settled on the stool, pulling out money as the man fixed their drinks. "You ever run the Mariposa?"

"Nah. Too far and crazy for me, man. I was always a rambler." He put the drinks down in front of them. "That'll be $6.50."

James paid and picked up his drink. "Thanks." He pointed to a booth in a dark corner, and they headed over there, slid into the anonymous gloom. The room smelled of a hundred years of tobacco soaked into old wood and beer spilled a thousand times on the floor, of bar cleaner and patchouli incense, which was oddly appealing. "Do you want to play some music?" he asked Miranda.

"Sure. Let's choose together."

He grinned. "Okay."

They walked over to the jukebox and flipped through the tunes, laughing at the possibilities. "I don't even know half this stuff," Miranda admitted. "But I like the Beatles and the Rolling Stones."

"Everybody knows the Beatles and the Stones," he said. "Let's be more adventurous." Raising his head, he called out to the bartender, "What should we play for you, man?"

"Procol Harum, 'Whiter Shade of Pale', if you don't mind," he said, wiping down the bar. "I fell in love to that song, once upon a time."

"Got it." Miranda wanted Janis Joplin, a song he didn't know called "Turtle Blues" and he chose a couple of Santana tunes his dad always loved. Then he said, "Pick something for no reason except it sounds cool."

Miranda chewed her lower lip, and her hair fell down beside her face, lit from beneath. "Velvet Underground is a cool name."

He punched the numbers. As the music came on— not too loud, which he appreciated—he grinned at Miranda. "This place is great. Thanks."

"My pleasure. I found out about it one night right after I got here. I've been meaning to come here ever since. It's like a time warp."

He looked around. "No, I could take you some places that are time warps. This one is just retro, nostalgic."

She nodded. "I'd agree with that." She faced him, arms crossed on the table. "So where would we go in Albuquerque? Tell me about your town."

Her eyes shone in the dim light, and her mouth framed an invitation with every word she spoke, and he wanted to see her laugh, so he said, "Well, if you want to go back in time, we could head on over to Joe's White Horse, which was probably sitting right on that corner when Pancho Villa was riding, and I'm pretty sure nobody has ever mopped the floor since." He sipped his soda. "Of course, you would need to bring a pistol."

He was rewarded with her low, earthy chuckle, a sound that vibrated all the way down his spine. "It sounds like something out of that movie *Desperado*."

It startled him. "You know that movie?"

"I *love* that movie!"

"No kidding! Me, too." The idea he'd been forming of her—a bit of an intellectual, a cosmopolitan, maybe a tiny bit of a snob—shuffled around to fit this new bit of information. "I'm surprised you do, though—it's really bloody."

"Yeah," she agreed. "But it's cartoony. It's so campy." She raised an eyebrow, acquiescing to the obvious with a one-shouldered shrug. "And it doesn't hurt that Antonio Banderas wears pants with silver buttons."

"Ah," he said, "the mariachi look can be done, *señorita*."

The smile that edged across her mouth then, slow and knowing, just about knocked him out. "I might take you up on that, *señor*."

A Rolling Stones song came on and the bartender whooped and clapped his hands. "Time to dance, folks!" He rolled out to a postage-stamp-size square of floor toward the back of the room, and started dancing beneath a ball that flashed yellow, orange and blue in slow, globby flower patterns.

Miranda laughed. "Far out, man." She stood up and held out her hand for James. "We can't leave him out there dancing all alone."

"I'm a terrible dancer."

"Men always say that. I don't care. No one else will, either."

They were not the only ones drawn by the exuberance of the bartender, who was obviously the owner. Some of the backpackers and a couple of the biker couples joined him, too. James, feeling awkward, joined in as well as he could, if only for the sheer pleasure of watching Miranda dance.

She had graceful arms she used like a hula dancer's, and a naturally sinuous swaying form that drew the eye down her long, slim form. Beneath the shifting lights, her skin took on one color after another, as if she were a painting, and her hair swayed and flowed, her eyes glittering in great fun as she looked up at him.

Then the bartender's song came on, and Miranda slowed to a twirling flower, drawing him in and around her. He did his best to follow, smiling at her encouragements, knowing he probably looked like an idiot, but it didn't matter, because no one—male or female— could possibly look at him while Miranda was there, burning, a flame, a painting, a scarf floating on currents of music.

He had never seen anything so beautiful in his life.

And he knew that her dance was for him, to coax him, capture him. Hypnotize him. Make him her slave.

He might once have believed in love, or seen a woman he thought was beautiful. He had not. As long as he lived, he would remember these moments when Miranda danced to Procol Harum and then "White Bird," washed in color, in sound.

They were sweating. The swell of her breasts was washed with perspiration that glistened yellow, blue, white, and he lifted a finger to trace a line through it, just one finger. Her eyes turned dark as he lifted her sweat to his lips and tasted it. Her nostrils flared, and her lips parted—consciously or unconsciously?—and she ran a hand down the length of her hip.

And then, the song was over, and something loud and raucous came on, something a lot of others must have approved of, because customers crowded the floor. Miranda and James were shunted off to a dark corner, and there, against a velvet curtain that must have come from an old-fashioned movie theater, he pressed into her, taking her mouth with all the passion he wanted to expend between her legs. She wrapped her arms around him and pulled him—hard, so much strength!—into her body, arching so her breasts crushed into his chest. Their legs slid together, scissor-style, so the yearning, over-heated, throbbing parts of them were pressed together in promise of the relief they could offer, one to the other.

She tasted of sweat and beer and something hot he thought must be her own flavor, because it heated and intensified as they kissed, her tongue and his sliding together, and around, along each side, front to front and back and away to corners of a lip, to the bow.

He was madly, painfully, intensely aroused, and it took everything in him to shove his hands in her heavy weight of silky red hair, next to her damp skull, and pull himself away. Hold her away so he could look down at her eyes.

She stared up at him, her chest rising and falling against his, arousal and exhaustion. "Holy…damn," she said, and swallowed. "I'm not—" she floundered for words "—you are…this is…"

"Hot," he said, and brushed her hair away from her face.

"What will we do about it?" she challenged.

Something in the jutting angle of her chin made him realize it meant more to her than she'd let on. There was more innocence in her than she wanted to claim. She played the cynic, but who was a cynic other than a fallen romantic? To disbelieve, one had to once have had faith.

So he gave her a grin and told a half-truth. "For a few days, we'll just dream, hmm? I have a race to run."

"You mean, you can't…when…?"

"Can't is a strong word." He felt himself coming under control and pulled away from her gently. Under cover of the crowded dance floor, they got back to their seats. "If I want to win, it's better to save my energy. Even…build it up."

She tossed her head in saucily. "So, you're just using me to heat up your machine, huh?"

He laughed. "Only because you are very, very good at it."

Sliding into her seat, she grasped her beer and took a long gulp. "Glad to be of service."

He, too, drank deeply of his soda and glanced at his watch apologetically. "Speaking of that run, I need to get back—I need to get a jog in tomorrow morning, stay loose for Saturday. Can I walk you home?"

A softness bloomed in her dark blue eyes. She nodded. "That would be nice."

He lifted a hand at the bartender on the way out. "'Night, guys," he called. "Have a good one."

The night was cool and starry, and as they headed into the residential district, it was also astoundingly quiet, the trees swishing in a high breeze, a faraway dog barking at some imagined creature in the hedges. Through the windows, they could see living rooms, dining rooms. Televisions flickering blue, heads on couches. An old woman sat on her porch with a dog at her feet. "Evening," she said, her voice carrying easily across her damp grass to the sidewalk where they walked.

James held Miranda's hand and felt like he was in a play, in an imaginary world conjured up by some fifties television show. "This place is unreal," he said.

"It is," Miranda said, shaking her head. "I think that every time I come here. It's almost like it wants to seduce you or something."

"Yes."

She walked quietly beside him. "Desi says that the lady of the mountain calls certain people here."

"That's what they say about Taos, too. And other people hate it. Hard to imagine anyone hating this place, though."

"People do, though." She paused. "This is my sister's house. Or at least it will be her house for another week or so."

He halted, but didn't let go of her hand. Looking at the window instead of her face, tilted up toward his, he said, "Miranda, this has been one of the best days I've ever had. I mean that seriously. Thank you."

Her husky voice said, "Me, too." Raising on her tiptoes, she kissed his cheek. "Good night."

He let her go. "Sweet dreams, Miranda."

Inside Miranda found Juliet asleep on the couch, Josh's silly soft red dog snoring beside her. The television flickered without sound, and there were stacks of shower thank-you notes ready to be addressed. Feeling buoyant and alive, Miranda silently picked them up and carried them over to the table where another stack, already hand-addressed, awaited stamping. It was pretty easy to see where Juliet had left off. She made a cup of tea and bent over the task. A small thing she could do.

Juliet started awake about twenty minutes after Miranda had come in, and stiffly sat up. "How long have you been here?"

"A while. Why don't you go to bed properly? You need your beauty sleep."

She shook her head. "If you don't mind too much, I think I'm going to go sleep with Josh. It's getting harder and harder to sleep in my own bed, without him. It's just…not right."

"I do not mind in the slightest. I was surprised you were sleeping here anyway."

"We want the wedding night to be special, to have a marker."

"Then I think you have to stay here tonight, sweetheart."

Juliet looked ready to cry. "I have nightmares sometimes."

"About the rape?" Miranda moved to sit beside her sister on the couch, rubbing her shoulders lightly. Juliet bore it better than usual—none of the girls could manage casual touching very easily. Their mother had been so very terrible about it. It felt odd to Miranda to be rubbing her sister's shoulder blades, but she kept it up anyway, her hands feeling hot, as if they had medicine in them. And who knew? Maybe they did.

Juliet sighed. "Yeah." She rubbed her face with both palms. "Yes. My therapist says it will get better as time goes by, and honestly, it is, but sometimes—one shows up. Less often when I'm sleeping next to Josh."

Miranda smiled. "If I were a nightmare, I wouldn't want to cross Josh, either."

Juliet laughed, and then to Miranda's complete surprise, she turned and gave her a big, hard hug. "Thanks, Mirrie. Maybe I can handle staying here if you're here."

For one fleeting moment, Miranda felt the comfort of her sister's arms without fear, a safe and solid place where she might, if she required it, land. And Juliet would catch her. An unnamable emotion welled in her heart, closing her throat for a long moment, and Miranda—mistaking it for fear—pulled away in hasty panic. "Is there…um…anything you want me to do in the morning? I'm going to stop by and see Desi, of course, and I'm going to meet the sari guy sometime in the early afternoon, but I'm happy to run errands or whatever you need."

Juliet gazed at her sister for a moment, then brushed a strand of hair from Miranda's forehead. "You have the best hair of all of us. Desi's is nice, but yours is like a magic cloak or something."

"If it was, I would long ago have used it to make myself invisible."

"No," Juliet said, smiling gently. "You never wanted to be invisible. You want to be *seen*."

Stung, embarrassed, Miranda pulled back. "No, I didn't. Don't."

"Nobody who wears her red hair to her rear end is trying to be invisible." Juliet grinned. "Nobody who wore a purple tutu and red fishnet stockings to school wanted to be invisible. Nobody who—"

"Okay, okay!" Miranda had to laugh. You might be able to posture around a lot of people, but a sister always called your bluff. "Maybe not."

"It was because of our parents, of course. They ignored you, Mother and Daddy."

"Except when they didn't."

"Right." Standing, Juliet yawned. "We should get some sleep so we can deal with them cheerfully tomorrow."

"I'm pretty sure I can't do cheerful. I will strive, very hard, for civil."

"I can live with that." She picked up a piece of paper and peered at it. "Oh, I forgot—your skier called again. Where did you go anyway? You've been gone forever."

"Um…" She smiled, abashed and trying not to show it. "I ran into James Marquez at the grocery store and we went up to the top of the mountain for a while. Then had a beer at The Poppy Seed." Unconsciously she stroked her mouth, thinking of the light blazing off his shiny dark hair, the taste of his lips, the endearingly awkward way he moved his hips on the dance floor.

"Not a drop of chemistry, though, huh?" Juliet grinned.

"Well. Maybe one or two."

"He seems like a nice guy." She yawned again. "The skier is quite insistent that he needs to see you, too. Feast or famine, huh?"

"I guess." Miranda took the paper with Max's number. "Did he say what he wanted?"

"Just that he had some things he needed to tell you and if you wanted to meet him tomorrow to give him a call." She glanced at the clock. "Probably not at one-thirty."

Stunned, Miranda stared at the clock. "Oh, my gosh! How did it get so late?"

"Time flies when you're having fun."
"We need to go to bed."
"I think I said that."

Chapter 10

James had left several messages for various people in town the day before, and when he returned from his long, slow jog the next morning, there was a stack of messages waiting for him at the desk. He leafed through them as he rode up to his room, arranging them in order of importance. A judge wanted to buy him a cup of coffee, talk about the land issues surrounding Desi's land. Important. The cops had decided to talk to him about the evidence they'd collected—he grinned—a favor he'd called in from a senator, a guy he'd gone to school with.

And shockingly, Christie Lundgren, the skier, had agreed to meet with him as long as he didn't bring Miranda.

Fair enough. He punched in Christie's number

before he even took a shower, and arranged to meet her in the coffee shop at the top of the mountain—her suggestion, not his—in an hour. He called the sheriff and agreed to meet the deputy in charge of the case at eleven, and then, frowning, he looked up the judge's name in his notes. Judge Yancy, the old judge who had offered to marry Desdemona after the murder, who seemed to be part of the land grab perpetrated by Biloxi and maybe some other shadow partners.

He also made a note to himself to check out the science behind the aquifer beneath the land. If it was worth billons as some of the articles said, a whole lot of people might be willing to kill for it.

Stripping off his sweaty vest and running shorts, he jumped under the shower. It was where he usually did his best thinking, in the shower, after a run. This morning, his head was packed with the silky red hair of a siren who'd danced him senseless the night before. All night, he'd tossed and turned, his body a furnace, thinking of her mouth, her delicate hands, her—

That was the trouble getting mixed up with a client. He couldn't think straight. And somebody's life was on the line if he couldn't find out who really killed Claude Tsosie and why. Rubbing his body dry, he wondered grimly if the "accident" yesterday had even been an accident. And a hit-and-run was an awfully big coincidence under the circumstances. And if it wasn't, then this was a lot bigger than a love triangle.

If it was a land grab worth billions, Desi's best course of action would be to sell the land to the gov-

ernment with stipulations of leasing and energy or
water rights into perpetuity. He had a feeling only the
government could protect her properly. When that
much money was at stake, people would do anything.
He needed to talk to her about the possibility.

He dressed in a simple white running T-shirt and a
pair of khaki shorts, and stopped to comb his hair in the
mirror. As he met his eyes there, he told himself the
other thing he had to get done was to tell Miranda the
truth about why he'd left the seminary. He didn't kid
himself—this had the potential to be a serious connection, and he wanted everything out in the open.

Christie Lundgren was a pretty woman, and she was
irritably fending off the advances of a square, muscular
hiker when he arrived at the Top O' the Mountain
Morning coffee bar. It wasn't his kind of place—too
midcentury with all those little squiggles on parchment
looking glass and mod-looking leather chairs. But he
wasn't here for the decor.

"Hello, Christie," he said, gesturing toward the seat
next to hers. "I hope I am not late."

"No, right on time." She glared at the athletic youth
and he slunk away with a shrug.

"Can't blame a guy for trying," he said.

"I guess." She gestured to the barista, who hurried
over. "Do you want something?"

They ordered, plain coffee for James, a chai with soy
for Christie. "So what do you want to talk about?" she
asked.

"Let's move over to the window, huh? Little more privacy."

When they were stationed on tall chairs overlooking the view of the San Juans all around them, sunny and brilliant in the morning, he said, "I just want to find out who really killed Claude. Desdemona Rousseau didn't do it, and I think you know it."

Christie lowered her eyes. "I don't know if she did or didn't. I think there are things the police haven't bothered to ask about."

"Yeah? Like what?"

"Like why are his paintings worth so much?" She twisted her mouth in disdain. "Have you seen them?"

"No."

"They're not bad," she said. "But it's not like he was some great artist. And he hadn't even been painting for that long, really. Only a few years. So why the big excitement?"

"Good question," he said. "*Very* smart question. You have any ideas?"

She shook her head. "It just crossed my mind a few times. I heard somebody paid a hundred grand for one. That's just crazy."

"Anything else you can think of?"

She took a long swallow of her chai, and looked into the distance. He saw the pain around her mouth and touched her arm. "It has come to my attention that he might have had a lot of women, not while he was with me, but before. While he was married."

"Anybody in particular?"

"This wacko woman who is married to a dentist around here. They have tons of money, but she acts like—" She shook her head. "I don't know what. She's crazy. Alice something. She has—or had—a bunch of his paintings, too, and I think she sold some of them on the Internet."

Her sorrow and pain and regret came radiating from her in almost visible waves. James waited.

"I really did love him, you know," she said quietly. "Maybe it wasn't right or whatever, but I didn't date him even one time before he left his wife. He chased me for ages, and he was really smart and beautiful and he seemed to *see* me, you know?" She raised her eyes. "I think he loved me for real."

Kindly, because it would not hurt anyone for him to say it just this minute, he said, "It sounds like he cared a lot for you."

She nodded. "Have you ever had a really terrible broken heart?"

"It's the worst," he said. "And I'm not going to tell you to get over it. Just let it be broken for a while."

A single heavy globe of a tear rolled out of her right eye. She nodded. "I don't think Desi killed Claude. She was mad at him, but I think maybe she really loved him, too."

"I think she did," he agreed. "Listen, what do you know about the connection between Renate and Elsa?"

Christy frowned, obviously bewildered. "They're sisters. I knew them in Europe, with Max." Suddenly she looked troubled.

"What is it?"

But she shook her head. "Nothing. Never mind. If you need anything else, just call me," she said, and stood to put on heavy black sunglasses.

"Thanks." He watched her walk away, tense and strong, her blond curls almost unnaturally shiny. In time, she would get over Claude Tsosie and find another lover. She was young. She would be all right.

He would light a candle for her.

Miranda slept till nearly nine, and jumped out of bed in a tizzy. Juliet had left a pot of coffee and some store-bought cinnamon rolls and a note that said she'd be off work around noon. She ran a small nonprofit and had built a strong staff over the past six or eight months, so could afford to take time off as needed for the wedding. *Go see Desi,* the note urged, *and call me with a report. I saw her this morning, but there is a lot to do.*

She gulped the coffee, took a quick shower and then agonized over her clothes. She had brought little with her, but what if she had a chance to see James? It needed to be something beautiful. A blue silk tank seemed too fancy, a white T-shirt too low-key, a green peasant blouse entirely too sexy for meeting salespeople.

Finally, she settled on a simple shirtwaist dress made demurely sexy by the transparent floral print and an old-fashioned, forties-style slip beneath it. She wasn't a shorts kind of girl, and wasn't about to show off her paste-white legs in shorts in a town where everyone took their exercise in the outdoors. She'd look like a freak.

Smearing SPF 50+ sunscreen on every inch of exposed skin, she grabbed her purse and walked to the little hospital. The desk nurse directed her to a room on the second floor. When she got there, Tam was sitting next to the bed, reading aloud from some adventure story. He was a robust and wonderfully cheerful man, just right for the direct and sometimes gloomy Desi.

Speaking of Desi—Miranda's stomach flipped when she saw her sister lying there on the bed looking wan and bruised. Her face looked awful—purple and blue around her right eye—and her arm was immobilized in a temporary cast up to her shoulder. It always frightened her to see someone hurt badly, and the closer she was to the human, the worse it got. Her hands shook as she moved into the room, across the floor to Desi's bedside.

"Hi, honey," she said. "How are you doing?"

"I've had better days," she said with a wan smile. "But the baby is fine, so that's the important thing."

"Oh, I am so glad." She narrowed her eyes. "I think it's a very good thing there are saris on the way here. The scarf will offer a lot of possibilities. Not sure we can get even a sari around all this taping, though."

"I have to wear something!"

"We'll work it out. I'm supposed to report back to Juliet what's going on, so give me the scoop. I also need to know where you'll be later. Are you going home?"

Desi shot a mutinous glance at Tam. "No, actually. I'm not allowed to go home for another day or two."

"They want her to really rest," Tam said, raising an eyebrow. "And I told them she wouldn't if they let her go."

"You evil man, you." Miranda touched her sister's hand. "Is there anything you need for me to do?"

"Thanks, I'm fine, honestly. Everyone has pitched in very kindly. The wolves are covered and Helene now has the dogs."

"Want some magazines or books or something? I could bring my laptop in for you to watch movies on."

Desi brightened. "The movies would be great. I never have enough time to watch them."

In her purse, the cell phone rang. Miranda pulled it out and saw James's name. She didn't answer it, but a thrum of pleasure went through her when the message indicator trilled a minute later. To Desi, she said, "I'll give you a call when the guy gets here with the saris. And I guess I can give you some warning over Mother and Daddy, too."

"I'm really looking forward to this," Tam said, his Kiwi accent drawling.

"Oh, I'm sure we all are," Miranda said. "When are you going to tell her about the baby?"

"I guess I have to tell them now, since the doctors keep talking about it. They'll hear it and know anyway."

"That's a good idea."

A head popped around the corner. "Are you Miranda?" the nurse asked.

"I am."

"There's someone here to see you."

Miranda wondered who even knew she was here. "I'll be back."

Max, sturdy and blond and looking gigantic, waited in the plain chairs lined up against the wall. He rose when he spotted her, and objectively, she saw that he was a very attractive man, with gold hair glittering on his strong legs, those broad shoulders and classically handsome face.

But nothing in her responded to him at all. Not even the slightest quiver.

Uh-oh, said the voice.

Surprised, she sought out the details of him that had so thrilled her in Europe—the blue of his eyes, his big hands—and…nothing.

Uh-oh.

"Hi, Max. What's up?" she said. Surely when he spoke, that accent would catch her, charm her.

"I have only been trying to call you for most of these two days. I was worried about you, your sister."

Nope. Not even that gilded Continental accent could give her a shiver. She crossed her arms. "She's banged up, but she's okay."

"Will you come walk with me? I found out some things you might wish to hear."

"Really? Yeah, just let me tell Desi what's going on." She dashed back to the room, grabbed her purse. "I have to go," she said. "I'll explain later. Hey—you want a chai?"

"Now that sounds good. Thank you."

"Where would you like to go?" Miranda asked as they headed out to the brilliantly blue and gold summer day. "Have you tried The Black Crown?"

"I have not."

"It's only a few blocks. We can walk over there and have a cold drink."

"Very well."

Bizarre, Miranda thought. How could her grand passion just dry up and blow away like that? Was it as simple as chemistry?

The voice started to say *uh*—but she cut it off, slammed it into a box where it could go yell all it wanted without her listening. She was tired of thinking so much.

At The Black Crown, they took a seat in a booth near a bank of windows. Miranda ordered iced tea, and Max asked for lemonade. There were few customers so early—an obvious business sort at the bar, eating meat pie, a couple of girls chowing down on grilled cheese sandwiches, their packs at their sides. She thought, in a faintly distracted way, of how James said he'd never traveled that way. With his curious, open mind, he would enjoy it very much.

She realized she'd drifted off and brought her attention back to Max. "Sorry. I wasn't paying attention. What did you say?"

"The woman with dark hair there is Renate Franz."

Miranda eyed the woman curiously. Small, neat and dark, she had a great figure and good bones in her face. Probably close to sixty, but didn't look it unless you noticed her jawline. "How do you know her?"

"Christie introduced me last night at the hotel bar. Renate has come to town for her holiday. She likes to watch the runners."

Of course. Renate represented Claude's work, and Christie had probably met her in those circumstances. But a little light blinked on, too. "Did Christie know Renate in Bavaria?"

"I don't know."

Miranda nodded. The whole thing kept getting more and more tangled, like a maze with no outs. That was why Bavaria had rung a bell when she talked with Max before. "So what did you learn?"

"Not a lot, Miranda, but I offer it in goodwill."

"Okay."

"Claude lived in Bavaria for a long time. Not just a student period. Years."

"Doing what?"

"I do not know that. Christie said he spoke perfect German with a Bavarian accent."

Miranda had not spent tons of time with her dead brother-in-law. He and Desi met around the same time Miranda flew the nest, and she had not been around him a lot. Mostly she'd liked him. He'd been charming, intelligent, easy to get along with. She knew he'd spent time overseas, as a student and in the Peace Corps, which is where he and Desi met. "Hmm. But that would make sense if he lived in Bavaria, right?"

"I suppose," Max said.

Except, somehow it felt wrong. How did a guy like that, raised in the barrio in Denver—and he'd often made much of his ghetto childhood—get the chance to go to Europe? It didn't add up.

Suddenly she realized she was missing a fantastic opportunity. "Max, will you do me a favor?"

"Yes. Anything."

"Introduce me to Renate, then make up some appointment you have to keep so I can talk to her. Don't say my last name."

"I was hoping we might have lunch, Miranda. I was hoping you might give me another chance."

"Sorry," she said. "That's just not ever going to happen."

"I was an idiot to let you get away," he said with what sounded like genuine remorse.

"Maybe," she said, "but maybe we are just not right for each other." Reaching across the table, she took his big hand. "Can we be friends? I do so like your company."

For a moment, he looked at her, then squeezed her fingers. "Yeah, sure. Friends."

"Good. Now introduce me to Renate, and remember, I'm an artist from New York City."

Renate looked up with a pleasant expression when Max approached, including Miranda in her smile. "Hello."

Max spoke in German, and at first, Miranda was afraid of what he was saying, but that was silly. He gestured to Miranda, and she heard her name, but nothing else.

"So you are an artist?" Renate said, pushing her plate away so she could put her hands on the table.

"Yes. I've been to your gallery in Manhattan. It's wonderful."

"Please, sit down. Tell me about your work."

"I have to go," Max said, and bent to give each of them polite kisses on both cheeks. "Call me, Miranda, and we will have a lunch before I go to New Zealand."

"I will, Max. Thank you."

He raised a hand in farewell. Renate politely focused on Miranda, who suddenly felt clammy. What would she say? What did she want to find out?

Anything that would help, she realized. Brushing hair from her face she said, "I'm mainly a sculptor," she said, "with a sort of whimsical style."

"Yes. Have you a gallery you work with?"

It wasn't a lie to say, "Not at the moment. I was working with a woman who died, and the son didn't want to continue."

"Not Rosa Hart?"

"It was," Miranda said. "We worked together a long time."

"Well, give me your card, and we will meet again in the city. Will you like that?"

"Of course. Yes. I don't actually have a card on me, but I'll be glad to bring you one, or I can call you when we go back to the city."

"That would be fine."

Now what? Miranda hadn't got anything! "I saw the Tsosie exhibit a few months ago. Did it do well?"

"Very well. Native American art is extremely popular now, which is why I come to Mariposa on my holiday. Often, I have found good work at the craft shows here."

"The Tsosie work seemed to really take off after his death. Did you help create that demand? It seemed so smart." Stupid, Miranda thought. And leading.

But Renate straightened a bit. "The story added a layer of—" She struggled with the word. "Magic? Mystique."

"I can see that would be true. Did you know him very well? I seem to remember reading he spent time in Bavaria, is that where you met?"

Renate frowned. "Were you his lover?"

"God, no!"

"I knew him well, since he was a child. I think, had he lived, he would have made a big mess of his life and there would have been no more art."

"What, like drugs or drinking or something?"

She shook her head. "Women. He had a weakness for women."

Miranda lifted a shoulder. "Well, he obviously pushed somebody too far finally, didn't he?"

"Yes. It is too bad," she said, but it was rote, not meant. Her eyes narrowed suddenly. "What was your name, please?"

"Miranda Rousseau." Only after she said her whole name did she realize her mistake. So much for playing private investigator.

"I thought so. You are the sister of Claude's wife, is that right?"

Miranda hesitated, but there was nothing to be gained by lying. "Yes. Desi Rousseau is my sister."

"I do not want to speak with you any longer."

Miranda stood, partly to keep Renate from running away, partly out of respect. "I'll go in one minute. But it seems like you might know something, or maybe your sister—"

"What sister?"

"Elsa. She told us that you are."

The art dealer's face went very still. "I see." Her graceful hands rested on her forearms. "What do you want?"

"I just want to think about this a little. Claude led her on a merry chase, and she didn't deserve it. Now she's fallen in love, she's happy and she's going to have a baby and all that needs to happen is for everybody to come forward with the information they have so that she can get on with her life." She tossed hair over her shoulder. "Doesn't that sound fair?"

"I did not know she was pregnant. And I thought the charges would be dropped by now."

"They haven't. If you would just go tell the police what you know, it might really help."

"I will think about it."

In her purse, Miranda's phone rang and she suddenly remembered the sari guy. She held out her hand. "Thank you for giving me this time. I have an appointment. Thanks for your time, Ms. Franz."

"I am still interested in your work. Call me when you return to New York."

"I will. Thank you." She rushed out and on the sidewalk, yanked her phone out of her pocket and looked at the name. It was Naagesh and Sons Imports, and she stabbed the number in. When a man answered, she said breathlessly. "I'm sorry. This is Miranda Rousseau. I'm here. Do you have the saris?"

"I do. Can I show them to you?"

"Yes. Where are you?"

"I am at the Hotel Mariposa, in the lobby."

"I'll be right there." She slapped the phone closed, and dashed the two blocks to the hotel, hoping she wasn't looking too rumpled in case she ran into James. She paused for a moment, brushing hair into place, smooth her skirts, and she even took a second in the blazing sun to put on her lipstick.

A butterfly danced nearby and she smiled. James must be about somewhere. Smiling happily at both the possibility of finding a beautiful sari for her sister and seeing James, who might just be her lover someday soon, she pushed through the giant doors of the old hotel, into the light air-conditioned lobby.

She spied a dark man with an armful of gilded scarves first. She waved and headed toward him.

"Miranda! Aren't you going to say hello, darling?"

She whirled, struggling to keep the dismay off her face. "Mother!"

Chapter 11

Carol Rousseau was a New England blue blood, and looked it. Her hair was smoothly cut into a sleek, dark pageboy she could let swing or gather into a ponytail for a game of tennis or sweep into an updo with glittering jewels tucked into it discreetly. Her figure was not an ounce over what it had been the day she graduated from high school, and she had no tolerance for anything less. She found fat vulgar.

Today she wore a yellow cotton suit with short sleeves, and a jaunty little boater hat on her head. "You look wonderful as always, Mother," Miranda said, bending to kiss her cheeks Continental fashion as she insisted upon. With Max, she didn't mind. With her mother, it grated.

"Where's Daddy?"

"He's gone to take the car around." She peered at Miranda. "You've been in the sun too much again, haven't you? I'm starting to see sun damage around your eyes."

"I have sunscreen SPF 50 on, Mother," she said. "I'm not sure what else a person can do."

"Wear a hat, darling." She touched her own.

"I'll think about it," she said. "I need to talk to that man over there for a few minutes. I'll come find you when I'm done. Will you excuse me?"

"Of course, dear."

Miranda dashed across the room, smarting even though she knew better than to expect anything besides criticism from her mother. She hurried over to the man with the scarves and took no small amount of satisfaction in knowing how much her mother would hate the fact that the bridesmaids were so errantly dressed.

James spied Miranda's hair from the elevator, and—ridiculously, joyfully—his heart leaped. He made his way through the lobby, crowded with more runners and their relatives, and vacationers in expensive resort wear, homing in on Miranda. It seemed as if a shaft of light fell on her, but when he blinked, he realized it was only his eyes that saw her that way.

She was wearing the most amazing dress. Sheer enough he could see the straps of her undergarment, and buttons all the way up the front that he instantly imagined undoing, one at a time. She was admiring a fall of pale pink and green fabric, woven through with threads of gold, and although he thought it beautiful, he hoped she wasn't choosing that particular color scheme for herself.

He came up beside her. "Hello, little girl. Is that for you?"

"Oh, God, no. I'd look terrible in these colors. It's for Desi. What do you think?"

He nodded at the man who'd brought the saris, and shrugged. "I have no idea, Miranda. This is not my area." He pointed at a length of blue silk on the chair. "That color would look beautiful on you, I think."

"Think so?" She picked it up and draped the gossamer, embroidered scarf around her neck backward, letting the hems trail behind her. She put out her hands. "Do you like it?"

James swallowed. The blue in the scarf picked out the blue in the flowers on her dress, which drew his eye to the lace edging on whatever it was underneath the dress, and her breasts, moving with her arms.

"Beautiful," said the salesman.

"Yes," James said. He imagined the scarf over her white body, with nothing else on it, and urgently wanted to make it true. "I'll buy it for you."

"Don't be silly. I have pots of money my grandmother left me. Save your money."

Stiffly he backed away. "Okay."

"Oh, James, I'm sorry, that sounded careless and rude and—" She broke off. "Sorry."

"It's okay," he said, even though it wasn't. There

was, suddenly, a giant hole in his gut, that thing that told him how foolish he was for longing for things so far out of his reach. Not only beautiful, not only well-traveled, but rich, too. "I'll wait for you in the bar over there."

She looked at him for a moment. "Okay." To the man she said, "I'll take the pink and the blue," she said.

In the bar, he was sorely tempted to order just one beer. It might ease the sting of that careless rejection, and help him sleep later. But the race was in the morning and he'd just as soon have the best chance he could. There were schools of thought that said a beer would be all right, but he noticed the difference in his body when he had one and when he didn't.

He settled next to an older man with the clean jaw and good shoes of a yachtsman. "How're you doing?" he said.

"Fine, fine. You here for the run?"

"Among other things." He eyed the man's rangy leanness, the sun-freckled forehead. "You, too?"

"Yeah, well, we'll see how I do. It's a tough run, especially for an old dog like me."

"Better to run than not."

"I reckon so." He sipped a clear drink.

James ordered a soda water with lime and waited for Miranda, eyeing her as she paid the man for the clothes. He grinned, showing very white teeth, and saluted her as he left, whistling on his way out. Obviously well paid.

Miranda came toward the bar, and he saw the cynical

tightness in her mouth, but felt no urge to erase it. Her arms full of clothes, she came into the bar, shaking her head.

The man next to him stood, a little formally, and said with genuine pleasure, "Miranda, girl! You're a sight for sore eyes, as always."

Politely she kissed his cheek. "Hello, Daddy. You're looking well." She drew James into the circle with a gesture. "This is James Marquez. He's helping us figure out the Claude business."

The man held out a hand, his gaze direct, his grip firm. Miranda said, "James, this is my father, Paul Rousseau."

James halted midshake and blinked. "The poet?"

"God love you, boy. Yes."

"I've read everything you've written, sir," James said honestly, an attack of hero worship filling his lungs. "Poems, short stories, the essays on running for the *New Yorker,* the travel pieces in the *Atlantic*—" He paused, feeling idiotic. "I love your work. Very much."

Rousseau smiled. "Thank you, son. As a runner, you're probably in tune with some of the same things I am."

"Right." He felt flummoxed, pleased. Also conscious of Miranda standing beside him radiating a tense, weird energy. He gave her a glance, and she met it with a heavy-lidded blink. "You might appreciate this, sir," he said to her father. "I met Peter Bok when I first got here the other day."

"No kidding. Didn't he set the record for this race?"

"Whoa, whoa," Miranda broke in. "If you guys are

going to talk racing, I'm leaving. I'm going to take these back to the house and I can meet you here in an hour if that works?"

"Are you talking to me or our friend here?" Rousseau asked.

"I was speaking to James, but of course I will see you."

"Didn't Juliet set up a dinner somewhere?"

"I don't know. I haven't heard."

"She did." Rousseau glanced at his watch. "Six o'clock, so we can meet her beau. I thought you were going to be there."

James saw the panic on her face and said, "I'm really sorry, but I need her tonight. She's been helping me collate facts, and there's been a lot of information that's come in today."

Her expression of gratitude was reward enough. "I'll see you and Mother after dinner, how's that? And I'll be there to cheer you on tomorrow for the race. Shouldn't you have been here to acclimatize or something?"

"Our cabin is at eight thousand feet, sweetheart. I've been training all summer, but thanks for your concern."

Miranda wrestled with the clothes in her arms. For a moment, James was torn between helping her and staying to talk to a poet he had admired for years. Thinking of her uneasy relationship with her parents, however, he knew which side he'd better land on if he ever wanted the chance to talk with her again.

"Miranda, I'll help you carry those back. Sir," he

said, standing, "it was great to meet you. I hope we'll have a chance to talk more tomorrow."

"I'm sure we will. Good to meet you."

"Thank you," Miranda said as she dumped half the weight into his arms. "I have a lot to tell you."

"And I have a lot to tell you." As they walked down the sidewalk, thin plastic covering the silk, he said, "I didn't realize your background was so—" he floundered for the word "—high end."

She said nothing for a moment, and her face gave nothing away. "Is this going to be an issue between us?"

"Is there an us?"

Her irises were as liquid as mercury. "That's not a fair question."

"I think it's very fair."

"Why do I have to say first? Why don't you say? Is there an us?"

Suddenly he got it. She wasn't rejecting him; she was afraid of being rejected.

"Oh, yeah," he said. "From my end, the answer is yes."

She swallowed. Dipped her head. "Mine, too."

"Miranda." He touched her smooth, perfect jawline. "I meant it, last night. There's something here that matters. Let's see what it is, huh?"

"It goes both ways, though. You don't get to set all the rules."

"Okay, which means what?"

"Look, I'm sorry I hurt your feelings over the sari. But the truth is, it was just expedient. Here is a fact—

I have money. I have money of my own and I have a fat inheritance my very wealthy grandmother split among my sisters and I, and I'll probably have more when the poet and his wife kick the bucket. So, it was just expedient to say I'd pay for it when I'm sure you—"

"*Don't* have any?" He halted in his tracks.

She stopped. "Well, yeah."

"I'm hardly poor," he said stiffly.

"I'm sure you aren't."

"The thing is, you robbed me of the pleasure of buying you something by making the assumption that I couldn't afford it."

"I didn't mean to hurt your feelings."

"I know."

They stood on the sidewalk holding yards of bright silk, and Miranda wouldn't look at him. "This is crazy," he said. "I don't want to fight with you."

"Then get off your high horse and don't be so proud."

"I'll do that if you'll stop trying to be in control of everything."

Her head popped up. "I'm not doing that!"

"Oh, really?"

He saw the recognition dawn on her face. "I don't mean to."

"I'm sure you don't." He shifted the silk on his arm. "You know what I'd like to do, Miranda? I want to come with you to the dinner for your parents and see how the family dynamic works."

She looked positively horrified. "Why?"

"I want to know who you are."

Her entire body went still, which served to underline how she was always in motion. "This is kind of weird, James." She looked off toward the ski slopes, the top of the mountain, anywhere but his face. "We only met a few days ago."

"That's true," he said. And left it at that.

At last, she looked at him. "Okay. We'll go to dinner. But no fair thinking I'm a bitch, or fawning over my father. There are things you don't understand."

"Deal."

They took the saris to Juliet's house, and Miranda was parched and hot and faintly irritable. Juliet was nowhere in sight, but her big red dog, Jack, made an absolute fool of himself over James.

"Okay," she said, nudging him aside. "That's enough."

"He's cute," James said, chuckling, bending to scratch the dog's chest and sides with expertise.

"Do you want something to drink?" Miranda asked, pulling open the fridge. "There's soda water. I noticed you drink that a lot."

"Sounds good." The kitchen and living room were divided by an open counter and James sat on one of the stools. "We do need to touch bases. A lot of information came up today."

She settled across from him, leaving the counter safely between them. "I heard some things, too. You go first."

"I met with Christie Lundgren," he said.

Miranda blinked. "No kidding? That's pretty interesting. What changed her mind?"

"As long as you weren't around, she'd talk to me. And it was illuminating." He quickly recounted the highlights.

"So, who does she think killed Claude? The dentist's wife?"

"Maybe. I was intrigued by the art connection, actually." He explained Christie's confusion on Claude's art pieces.

"She made a good point—why would his work be so popular so fast? I mean, it happens, but not very often," Miranda said. "I have some more to say about that, but I'll hear all your material first."

James nodded. "I also used some connections to get the sheriff to let me look at the files for Desi's case, and there are some interesting things in there. For one thing, the car that nearly killed her appears to have had state license plates."

"It was a *government* car?"

"Looks like it."

"What else?"

"There's been a real effort to suppress the investigation and let Desi take the rap. The evidence against her is entirely circumstantial, except the blood on her clothes, and that's been explained by the fight they had earlier in the day. A lot of people saw that."

Miranda frowned. "So, do you think it's the killer, or somebody else?"

"I don't know, but my gut still says the killer is a woman. It could be, however, that somebody is using the situation as it crops up, probably because they want that land."

"What if," Miranda said, "it's all connected some-how? What if somebody wanted revenge on Claude and used the land as a cover?"

He nodded. "Quite possible."

"I met Renate Franz this afternoon, and I just pre-tended to be an artist who wanted to show in her gallery, and I asked about Claude. I think she knows something, too," she said, not realizing until that very moment that she did think so.

She sighed. "But how the hell are we ever going to catch somebody red-handed?"

"Won't. We have to set 'em up, figure out who it is, and see if we can get them to tip their hand."

"Sounds dangerous."

He lifted a shoulder. "Maybe a little." He sat back and measured her. "I would like to go to the hospital and talk to your sister Desi about the land. Do you think she's up to it?"

"We can try." Brusquely she picked up their glasses, put them in the sink. "I need to run a comb through my hair first. And I need to gather some things to take to her."

He stood up. "Wait a minute."

She paused, touching her face, thinking she must have something on it. "What is it?" she asked, touch-ing her mouth.

"This," he said, and slid a hand around her neck. "I need to kiss you."

"Oh!" she managed before he was doing just that, his mouth claiming hers with elegance and knowledge, his hands on her neck, and arm, his thumb tipping her chin up.

Heat raced through her body, tweaking her breasts to sharp points that wanted his hands, swelling her sex to readiness for him, for the actions that were mimicked by his tongue now rolling around her mouth, filling her, coaxing her closer.

She melted against him, touching his long back, his strong arms. Against her belly was the hard nudging of his sex, and she rubbed against it, acknowledging his arousal, and he groaned softly. "This dress," he said in between kisses, rubbing his hands on the thin fabric, heating her skin. "This dress has been driving me crazy."

"Yeah?" she whispered.

He pressed his head to her forehead, looking down to where his hands moved on her shoulders. His fingers slid toward the edge of her slip, traced the lace that followed the shape of her breasts, halted. "It's so thin, so easy to imagine you not having anything on at all."

An inch, two, and his fingertips would touch the sharply tender tips of her breasts. She could feel the heat of his palms over her breasts, close but not touching. She made a soft noise and tipped her head up to kiss him, nipping his lips lightly. Her breath was high in her throat as he sucked her lower lip into his mouth, rubbing the tender flesh with his tongue, his fingers caressing up and down the slope of her chest. Up to her collarbone, down to the top of her slip. He suckled her lip, let go, nipped her lightly and rubbed the sting with his tongue.

Her brain turned to a puddle of sensation, and she just let him do what he would, waiting for the next thing, the slide and thrust of that tongue, the slow rocking of his hips below, the tantalizing hover and stroke of his hands that never, never quite touched her breasts.

At last, he gathered up her hair, and used it to tug her gently back to reality. "We have to go," he said.

"Do we?"

"Yes. But don't forget."

"No," she whispered. She backed away, turned on the water and splashed cold water on her face.

And that was only a kiss. Good grief.

He came up behind her and touched her shoulder, brushing her hair away to press a kiss to the back of her neck. "See, if you relinquish control sometimes, life can be interesting."

Miranda could not think of a single thing to say to that.

Desi had been moved to another room. She was desultorily flipping channels when Miranda and James arrived. She looked, Miranda thought, quite a lot better. Some color had returned to her face, and the general look of weariness was gone. She looked again like Desi—an annoyed, *bored,* Desi.

"Hey, you," Miranda said, coming in. "I brought you some things. First, the chai." She handed it to her with a flourish, a hot, steaming drink in a paper cup with its special sleeve. "Also, the computer and some DVDs to watch."

"Oh, you are my hero." Desi took the chai and inhaled the scent with her eyes closed.

"Where's Tam?"

"I made him go home. He's exhausted and hasn't slept since this happened." Her mouth turned up in a wry smile. "I'm sure he'll be back before long, but at least he'll have some supper and a rest." She eyed the fabric on Miranda's arm. "Is that my sari?"

"Yes! You remember James, right?"

"Sure. You catch the killer yet?"

"Working on it."

Desi nodded, then gestured to Miranda. "So—? Let me see it already!"

With a pleased grin, Miranda unfurled the luxuriously beautiful sari, pink banded with apple-green. The scarf was shot through with gold, and with a flourish, she draped it over Desi's torso. "What do you think?"

Desi squealed. Actually squealed. "It's fantastic, kiddo! You have such an eye! I would never have chosen these colors, but I love them."

"They look very nice on you," James said.

"Thank you." Desi put down her chai and held out an arm to her sister. "Come here and let me give you a hug."

Shyly, Miranda bent and allowed herself to be hugged. There was something homey—literally—about the way Desi smelled, and her heart lifted that she'd been able to do something to help. But she still felt awkward, and endured it only for a moment.

"Well done," Desi murmured.

As she straightened, she turned to include James.

"He'd like to talk to you about a few things to do with the case."

"Only if you feel up to it," James added.

"I'm fine. Well, I mean my brain and voice are fine."

He drew a chair forward and sat down. "Do you think Claude might have known about the aquifer under the land?"

Desi's eyebrows shot up. "I don't know," she said in a tone that said this was the first time it had occurred to her. "It's possible. He had some surveys done so we could dig the hot springs pool."

"Okay." James flipped open his notebook and tugged the lid of the pen off with his teeth. He made a note. "I'm going to tell you the honest truth—I know human nature. Whatever happens with this case, however it started, it's being fueled now by people who want that land, even if they were not responsible for Claude's murder."

"Okay," Desi said with a frown.

"You are not going to have a minute's peace as long as that aquifer is there, luring big money."

"Which means what?" Desi asked calmly. "That I have to sell it?"

"Might be the best answer."

Desi looked at her hands, and Miranda was surprised she didn't protest outright. "I'm listening."

"Here's the thing—if you don't sell it to the developers, you can probably find a lease agreement with the government."

"Ew. The government?"

"I've done a lot of work for my village back home,

negotiating contracts to rent land from the state government. If the government owns it, they protect it and their investment—and their law has a lot of teeth—but you can also work out a lease agreement with them, so you can keep the wolf sanctuary and your home and maybe even into the seventh generation."

"Is that a legal term?" Miranda asked, folding the scarf.

"No. Or a least not that I know of."

"They'll never pay me what it's worth," Desi said.

"Undoubtedly true. You could get more from developers. But I assume you've protected the land from them for a reason."

Desi nodded. "It's important to have some land that's not all built with million-dollar houses. The animals and trees need to live, too."

"I agree with you," he said calmly. "Here's the thing—the government is the only body that can really protect you. Once they own it, the deal is done, and nobody comes after you or your wolves anymore."

She gazed at him soberly. "I never thought about the possibility of leasing it back. I don't want to leave the land, but I am really tired of this struggle. I'm afraid—" She paused, then said more clearly, "I'm afraid that even if I don't go to jail, eventually somebody will succeed in killing me."

"That's my worry, too."

"That would suck," Desi said, and smiled. "I'll give it some thought."

"Don't talk about it yet, though, except with your fiancé."

"Okay." Desi shifted her attention to Miranda. "Hey, do you think you could do me a really big favor?"

"Sure. Whatever you want."

"Crazy Horse, the big white dog?"

"I know who he is!"

"Well, he's a big fat baby and he's really bummed out that Helene didn't get his special blanket." She winced and said, "Do you think you could drive up there and get it for her? She's working tonight."

"Of course! That's not even a big favor. It's very little." She grinned. "How will I know it?"

"It's a very hairy blue and red plaid that sits near the woodstove."

Miranda saw it in her mind very clearly. "I remember it. No problem. I'll run up there after dinner."

"So are you going to dinner with Juliet and Josh and the parents?"

"Yeah." Miranda widened her eyes. "James, darling creature, is going, too."

"You're a brave man." A sideways smile touched Desi's lips. "Glory and Mother should be an interesting combination."

"Yeah." The five-year-old was not known to hold her tongue. "Do they know about the baby yet?"

"Yes. They met Tam, too, just a little while ago." Her eyes glittered. "I can't wait to hear what Mother has to say about him later. She wasn't thrilled with his tattoos. And she's very upset about me having a baby out of wedlock."

"Well, it is kind of weird that you'll have the baby, but not get married."

"If I go to jail, I don't want him to feel obligated. I want him to find someone to love him and our daughter."

"*We'll* love him or her!"

"I know, Miranda. This makes sense to me, okay?"

"Okay."

"And where does *she* get off making judgments on other people?" Miranda exclaimed. "It's not like she's been some big model of morality."

"What do you mean?"

Miranda rolled her eyes. "All the affairs she and Daddy had, all their weird little games they played."

"Affairs? Really?"

And only then did Miranda realize she was too forthright, that her sisters did not know, had never known, the truth of things. The only reason she had the information was that she'd been subjected to their fights all those years. "Yes," she said, and cast a glance toward James, who probably didn't want to hear all this. "We'll talk later."

"Okay." Desi looked a little troubled.

"We'd better go. It's time for dinner."

Desi smiled. "I'll think about what you said. You guys have a real good time."

Juliet had arranged a reservation for all of them— Carol and Paul, Juliet, Josh and Glory, Miranda, Desi and Tam. Tam chose to spend the evening with Desi, keeping her company, so there was plenty of room for

James. The dinner was in the rustic, decidedly unposh Hungry Cattleman restaurant, which featured steaks and baked potatoes and baked beans. Homey.

She felt tense. Tired. Juliet directed them all to their places, and Miranda had to admit it was a brilliant design, meant to nip problems in the bud—on either side of Carol were Josh and James, two men she could flirt with. Next to Josh was Glory, then Miranda, then her father, then Juliet.

"This is quaint," Carol said. "Was it your choice, Josh?"

Josh, dressed in a crisp plaid shirt, his dark hair drawn into a shiny thick braid, mildly raised an eyebrow at Juliet. "Don't look at me."

"It's Glory's favorite."

Miranda looked at her niece-to-be, who gazed solemnly at Carol for a moment, then said, "You don't like it, do you?"

"Oh, no, dear. Of course I do. I just wish I'd been warned to wear jeans."

"It's the mountains, Mother," Miranda said. "A person might think to bring some jeans."

Carol held up the menu. "Well, yes, of course, but when one goes out to *dinner,* one doesn't think of that."

"I'm not wearing jeans," Glory said. "I'm wearing my pretty dress, so you don't have to feel bad."

The adults chuckled. Not Carol.

Just sitting there, Miranda felt the tension rising, both internally and externally. A thousand family dinners passed through her mind, when one or the other of the sisters had been the focus of Carol's sharp tongue and eternally dissatisfied eye. Most often, it had been Desi, who was too tall and round and serious for her mother's tastes.

"You do look wonderful, Mother," Juliet said, offering an olive branch. Behind her menu, she shot Miranda a glance that said, *help me keep the peace.*

"I agree," Miranda said. "Have you been working out?"

"Your mother has hired a personal trainer," Paul said proudly. "Best-looking woman in her age class by far."

"In my age class," Carol echoed, and it was as if her breath was blue freeze.

"Well, you know what I mean." Her father, Miranda noted, went very red in the cheeks. Unexpectedly she felt sorry for him. She looked back at the menu. "You always look great, Mother."

"Thank you, dear."

That was the worst of the evening. Everyone seemed to be on their best behavior. Miranda noticed her father wasn't drinking, and commented on it. "No martini, Daddy?"

"Not with a race in the morning."

Which gave James a chance to say, "Do you have a goal?"

"I can't win," Paul said, nodding. "But I'm hoping to end at the top of my age class." He cut neatly into his chicken breast. "How about you, son?"

James had a giant plate of spaghetti he was slowly

making his way through. "I want to win," he said, and smiled.

That smile knocked Miranda sideways. Slow, confident but not cocky, acknowledging the cheekiness of his intention while not discounting the possibility. An echo of warning moved through her. He wasn't just dangerous. He was mortally dangerous. Loving him could kill her.

"Can you do it?" Carol asked.

"Maybe. Depends on who is running with me."

"Good for you." She shifted her gaze to Josh, on her other side. "And will you run?"

"No. Never have been a runner."

"I see."

The conversation drifted, ebbed and flowed. They got through the appetizers and the salads, and Carol had only drunk a single glass of wine. When she ordered another, Miranda felt herself shrinking in her seat.

And sure enough, Carol found much to disdain as the meal went on. The bread was cold. The green beans were cooked to death. The waiter was too slow. The meat was tough.

Sometimes, Paul tried to ease things, joke Carol along, smooth the whole thing. Which generally made it worse. Maybe he'd learned that, because he didn't say a word to his wife, just let her bitch and moan about all the things that were wrong with the restaurant, the meal, whatever.

Mostly the rest of the company just talked around her. Then Juliet began to talk about various color schemes and flower choices for the wedding. In the midst of a description of the flowers for the altar, Carol cut in, "you can't mean to use lilies! They're funeral flowers."

"They're calla lilies and they're beautiful," Juliet said, smiling.

A few minutes later, Carol said, "I hope you're planning to get an updo or something for the wedding, Juliet. Your hair is looking a little thin to be wearing it long."

Woe be unto those who messed with the princess. For some reason no one could discern, Glory—age five— had gotten it into her head that Juliet was a princess, and nothing would dissuade her. Juliet was the greatest thing to land on earth. Ever. It was hero worship of the most profound sort, and she did not take kindly to Carol's tone.

"You're *mean!*" she said.

"Well, you're a rude little girl," Carol said without missing a beat. "You shouldn't speak to adults that way."

"Neither should you! My grandma says if you can't say anything nice, don't say anything at all."

"You didn't listen to her very well, did you?"

"Mother!" Juliet said.

"I know who you are," Glory said, drawing herself up to her full height, wiggling in the booster chair to be a little taller. "You're the wicked witch, aren't you?"

Chapter 12

For a long moment, silence engulfed the group. Under the table, James took Miranda's hand, and gave it a squeeze. She looked pale and strained, and he wanted nothing more than to whisk her out of there. This was obviously a very damaged family group, and while he still didn't know where, exactly, Miranda's need to be in control came from, he saw what must have been a highly difficult childhood. She clung to his hand as if it were a lifeline.

All at once, the whole group burst into laughter—and once they started, there was no stopping. It was laughter fueled with the gasoline of tension, and the more they laughed, the hotter the hilarity.

Carol stood stiffly. "I don't think this is even a little bit funny."

Juliet tried to stop laughing. "Mother, where is your sense of humor?"

"You need to rein that girl in."

Josh stood. "With all due respect, Dr. Rousseau, Glory was only responding to your tone. If you want kindness, that's what you have to give." He picked up his daughter, who looked close to tears, and cuddled her. "It's okay, honey."

Carol stiffly left the table and the restaurant. The others slowly sobered. Miranda took a big gulp of margarita and smiled with exaggerated cheer at her sister. "That went well."

"Could have been worse," Juliet agreed.

Paul Rousseau stood, placing his napkin carefully beside his plate. "I guess I'd better go patch things up. You all have a good night."

"Sorry, Daddy," Juliet said.

"Don't you apologize," Paul said, and pulled out his wallet and put some bills down beside Juliet's plate. "This is on me, too, so you young people just have a good time." With a wink at James, he said, "Especially you, young man. Party on."

James lifted his chin. "See you in the morning."

After he left, Josh sat Glory back in her chair. "It's all right, honey. Let's have dessert, huh?"

"Ice cream?"

"Sure." Josh looked around the table. "Who else?"

"None for me," James said, gesturing at the demol-

ished plate in front of him. He had his hand firmly on
Miranda's thigh, supple beneath the silky fabric of her
skirt. She smelled of oranges and spice, and he thought
the nightcap might be a cup of hot chocolate taken on
the balcony of his room.

"Me, either," Miranda said.

He took a chance. "Are you ready to go, then? Check
out the lead we talked about?"

Miranda looked at him. "Yes. I'm ready." She stood
up. "Sorry to bail, you guys, but now you can have your
dessert in peace."

"I don't like that lady," Glory said.

"I don't blame you," Miranda replied, and kissed her
on the head. "I'll see you tomorrow. Are you getting
your dress?"

"Yes. It's pink!"

"I can't wait to see it."

Watching, James wondered who had been so tender with these girls. They had a vast kindness in them,
all three of them did. It showed in Juliet's passion for
providing help and concrete services for the working
poor, in Desi's quest to save the wolves and he saw
it now in Miranda's gentle touch on the girl's head.
She did not hug her sister, he noticed, but patted her
shoulder.

"Don't wait up," Miranda said.

"I'm not sleeping there tonight. I'm too tense."

Miranda grinned. "Okay. See you tomorrow, then."

Outside the restaurant, it was still light out, with
heavy gold dripping across the skies and the rocky tops

of the mountains. The air was crisp, fine, light. Miranda let go of a gusty sigh. "Now what?"

"I have an idea," he said, taking her hand.

"So far they have proved to be very good. What did you have in mind?"

"The balcony of my hotel room. Room service hot chocolate and cookies."

She slowed. "But that seems a little too tempting, if you know what I mean."

"I have pretty good discipline."

"Maybe I don't."

"Maybe I have enough for both of us."

Something fiery blazed in her eyes. "That sounds like a challenge."

"Maybe," he said with a little smile. "Maybe not."

Her laughter was throaty. "All right, I'll go with you to your lair." She swung her handbag on her free wrist. "So, did you learn anything?"

"Your mother is an alcoholic. That can't have been easy."

"We don't call it that."

"Maybe that's part of the problem."

"At least part of it. The other part would be that she's the wicked witch." She laughed. "Oh, was that priceless?"

"She is not a very pleasant woman, that's for sure. Why is she so evil, though?"

"Oh, who knows, James? We survived her, that's all." She tickled his palm with her finger. "Can we change the subject, please? My mother has to be one of my least favorite topics."

They reached the hotel and Miranda scowled. "You need to do some reconnaissance, to make sure they're not in the bar. I don't want to deal with them."

He nodded, ducked into the hotel and looked around carefully, then went back out and took Miranda's hand. "All clear." He stopped by the concierge and asked for a pot of hot chocolate and cookies to be delivered to his room.

As they waited for the elevator, there was a soft space of awkwardness between them, the awkwardness of two bodies still unjoined. He found himself noticing the white corner where her neck met her shoulder, and thought about kissing it. Biting it. It would not take much to bruise that delicate skin—he would need to be careful.

He looked at her earlobe, reached up a hand to trace the shape of it and he drew a strand of hair between his fingers. "So soft," he said.

The elevator dinged and the doors slid open and they stepped into the gilded, mirrored box. A thousand Mirandas, a thousand hims. He stood beside her and admired the picture they made—she slim and white and pale, her hair a cloak around her shoulders, he whipcord lean and dark and sober looking, severe, like an old-time picture. He raised a hand to her neck, his fingers very dark against the alabaster paleness of her throat. She leaned backward, her head upon his shoulder, her eyes mere slits. He trailed downward, watching in the mirror as his fingertips slid over the skin revealed by her dress. Before his eyes, her nipples rose, and from this angle, he could see the lace of her bra.

With the tiniest smile, she pressed backward, her bottom rubbing his member ever so lightly, and he—

The bell dinged for the elevator, and the doors slid open. There was no one there. "This is our floor," James said, and pulled her off the elevator, and down the hall, both of them laughing.

His room was at the west end of the hotel, a corner with a view over the slopes. At night, he heard the trams moving over the mountain, moving, moving, moving, but it was worth it for the room. "Let me show you the view," he said, skirting the bed.

The French doors were open to the breeze, a light curtain rising and falling in flutters that made him think of that sari she'd purchased this afternoon. A vision of that thin blue fabric skimming her pale skin moved through his veins and he nearly shuddered.

They stepped out onto the balcony. Five floors below was the street, bustling with early evening traffic, back-packers and couples holding hands and families of sun-burned tourists headed for an ice cream. The tram moved up the hill relentlessly, shuttling weary workers and cheerful kids to the shops and apartments and the movie theater on the other side of the mountain. Miranda leaned on the wrought-iron railing and inhaled deeply. "Man, that's a good smell. Not like the city."

"The city doesn't smell good?"

"Not really. Especially in the summertime. It's

peculiar, and you do get used to it, but this—" again she took it in, her breasts lifting with the air in her lungs "—is really good." She tipped backward, leaning against his arm. "Are you planning to kiss me again, *señor?*"

"I could," he said, and did. He leaned into the siren call of her lips and tasted the summer flavor of margaritas. She moved closer, putting her body close to his, and he spread his hands over her back. They fit their lips and tongues together, kissing without urgency, and James took the time to imprint the feeling of her body against his, the uplifted pleasure of soft breasts against his ribs, the flare of her waist beneath his hands, the tense strength of her thighs pressing into his own. His blood simmered, just below boiling, where it had been for days—really since the first time he'd seen her.

He knew by the soft panting heat of her, the dampness of her skin and the low, hungry noises she made, that she felt the same way.

A knock sounded at the door. He raised his head, looked down at her. "Our hot chocolate."

"I like chocolate."

He went to the door and let the boy from room service in, carrying a tray with a big silver teapot on it, and cups, and a silver pitcher of cream, and a tray of beautifully presented cookies. He signed for it and showed the man out. When he turned back, Miranda was pouring the thick chocolate into cups. "Cream?"

"Yes."

"I'm worrying about your race."

"Don't." He put his cup down, settled on the chair and tugged her hand until she was in his lap. Gold light spilled through the open French doors, set her hair on fire. She rested on his lap, her feet still planted on the floor, as if she would run away. Smiling to himself, he pulled her knees up a little so her feet dangled over his legs. Demurely she sipped her chocolate, and he picked up his own cup.

"This is outrageously decadent," she said. "It makes me think of a place—" She halted and shook her head.

"Go ahead. It doesn't matter if you were with a lover. I don't mind."

"No, I wasn't, actually. But you seem not to like it when I talk about my travels. It bothers you."

"It doesn't bother me," he said, resolving to stop being such an ass. "Take me there. What does that chocolate make you think of?"

"Paris," she said simply. "A winter afternoon with a girl from Australia. We went to a little café and they served hot chocolate like this. We'd been walking all day and we were cold and wet and miserable and it was the best thing I'd ever tasted."

"I can imagine."

"You would like Paris, I think. It's so different from anywhere else. Just so itself, the light and the buildings and the carefulness of the Parisians, who are also very joyful."

He watched her lips as she spoke, watched the deep pink flesh shape words and taste her chocolate. "I would."

"Tell me another story," he said, admiring her throat. He put down his cup and put one hand on her thigh, another resting alongside her arm. She seemed a little taut, but giddy, too.

"What do you want to hear about? Ireland? Scandinavia? Spain?"

"Ireland. It seems a place I'd like." He stroked one finger down her arm, admiring the fine grain of her skin, almost poreless, so fine he could see tracings of blue veins beneath it. As he touched her, he saw that her nipples tautened, and although he was sure she didn't realize it, her buttocks and thighs tightened, shifted.

As she spoke of green fields bounded by hedges and white cottages and brightly painted buildings in the towns, he traced upward and downward on her arm. When he tired of that, he moved his hand down to her bare calf, and upward to her knee beneath the skirt. He traced the shape of it, touched the back of it, that sensitive place.

She put her chocolate down. Looked at him, waiting, all hair and lips. He slid his hand up her skirt, over a thigh as silky as water, all the way to her hip, to the edge of her panties at the side. She made no move to help him, and it was wildly arousing, a fact he suspected she knew. Her eyes were sultry, fixed on his face. She sucked her lower lip into her mouth.

He pulled his hand around beneath her skirts, skimming the skirt upward to reveal her thighs, long and fine and slim, and he moved his hand to the inside of her thigh, unable now to hold on to his composure as much as he would have liked, especially when she shifted, ever so slightly and spread her legs, pushing one thigh up against his arousal firmly.

He responded to her invitation by sliding his dark fingers over the milkiness of her leg, stopping short of the place she wanted him—his thumb or fingers or tongue—just in time. She moved against him, urging him upward, pressing her bottom closer to his sex, and he just stroked her thighs, looking at her mouth, her breasts.

She breathed in, and lifted her hands to her dress, and began, one at a time, to unfasten the buttons. With a little shimmy, the lacy undergarment shook right off her breasts and there were Miranda's pure white, supple, rose-tipped nipples.

Control, control, control. She wanted to control the situation because then she would not be afraid of him. He wanted to show her the joy in *losing* control. He leaned forward just enough to lick her right nipple, just once, then slid his hand a little way up her thigh.

"Please," she whispered, her breath coming more airily as he was poised above her breasts, breasts that his mouth watered to devour, skin that wanted his mouth on every inch of it. His control slipped and he pulled her close to him, shifting her so that she straddled his erection, her sex hard against him, and he opened his mouth and sucked her aroused nipple into his mouth.

She cried out, a mewling sound of pain and hunger,

and she grasped his hair, almost painfully. He grabbed her beautiful bottom in his hands and suckled and kissed and nipped her breasts until she was moving up and down against him, almost maddeningly.

Control, control. "Wait," he growled, and slid her over to the bed, urgently shoving up her skirts and practically ripping her panties from her, revealing that triangle of reddish hair. He held her still, suckling her breasts while he found the hot, wet center of her, and stroked her, fingers playing a tune she began to sing to, her head moving back and forth.

But with enormous control and more strength than he would have imagined she possessed, she turned the tables on him, taking advantage of a moment when he lost his head, pleased beyond imagining at the taste of her and the silkiness of her bare shoulders against his face, to shove him backward.

He laughed, and she grabbed his wrists in a grip that was stronger than he would have imagined. Tucking his wrists beneath her knees, she said, "Fair is fair." She pushed him down on the bed, and straddled him, the skirt of her dress making a pool around his waist.

With a saucy smile, she said, "Close your eyes for one minute."

"I'd rather watch."

"No." Inclining her head, she touched her own breasts, and he nearly fainted with the heat of it. "Close your eyes."

He closed them.

He could feel her doing something, but waited until

she said, "Okay, open them," that he realized she'd slid
the slip off from beneath her dress, leaving her naked
beneath it. No bra, no panties, just that floral fabric
hiding and revealing in equal measures. There was a
shadow of hair over her sex, and the pointed insistence
of nipples that wanted touching. As she bent to unbutton
his shirt, he glimpsed the white curve of a bare breast,
and he ached to touch it.

"I need to touch you," he said.

"Not yet, she said, shoving his shirt away from his
chest. Her hands skimmed over him, and she bent to
kiss his ribs, his belly, whatever she could reach without releasing his arms. "Beautiful," she murmured.

Then she slid just a tiny bit backward and unbuttoned her dress so that it fell just the slightest bit open
around her sex, and he groaned. She put her hands on
his belt and began to unfasten it, and James finally
gave in to the delight. He watched her, clad in diapha-
nous fabric and hair and sleek white skin, unbuckle him
and unzip him, and smile when she took his member
into her hand. "Oh, very nice," she said.

He felt her body relax the slightest bit, and flipped
her over. "My turn again," he growled, and she laughed,
the sound happy and full of life. He shucked his shirt,
and skimmed out of his jeans and there was Miranda,
lying below him in a puddle of late evening sunlight,
her hair spread like a magic fabric around her, her bare
breasts exposed by the opening of her dress, her legs
akimbo. He knelt over her and unbuttoned the dress.
"This is so pretty, let's be careful."

He divested her of the delicate fabric, then put her back on her back on the bed and looked down at her. She swallowed. "What are you doing?" she whispered.

"You are the most beautiful sight I've ever seen in my life," he said and knelt then between her legs and bent to gather her up, kissing her and feeling her legs anchor him, and then he plunged down and far away, into the waiting, hungry heat of Miranda.

Miranda gasped at the fierce plunge of James into her core at last. Every cell in her body quivered with the depth and heat of that charge, and she whimpered as he slowly, slowly pulled back, his tongue diving into her mouth as he plunged again, hard. She cried out in surprise and delight, and again, and again, and she tried to hold on longer, but an orgasm of monumental proportions split her right in half, the past and the future, and then James was following, over the edge, roaring and plunging, hard, hard, hard, bringing her to a place she'd never been, lost in so much pleasure it was like another being lived in her.

Then he collapsed with her, kissing her face, her neck, their bodies sweating and tangled. Slowly, a molecule at a time, she returned to her body.

And only then did she realize: "James! We didn't use a condom!"

His head jerked up. "Holy shit! How did we forget something like that? God, I'm so sorry."

"No, no. It's okay." But it wasn't. It was scary and weird that she'd forgotten. That she'd so willingly let go of everything that she forgot to use a condom. "I even have one in my purse!"

"And I have one in my pocket. It's even new."

Despite everything, Miranda laughed. "That was amazing," she cried, pulling him close, nuzzling his neck. "You made me completely forget everything, everything."

He rubbed the tip of his nose along her jaw. "Is that a purr, my little cat?"

"Oh, yeah." She looked at him, pulled his face up so she could see his dark, dark eyes, his long lashes, the sharpness of his conquistador's nose. "That was seriously the hottest sex I've ever had. Ever."

He smiled, nibbling her lip. "Good to know."

"Okay, you're missing your chance here, to say, 'me, too, Miranda.'"

His eyes glittered. "Sorry. Me. Too. Miranda," he said like a robot.

"Come on! Don't be mean to me."

His eyes went darkly sultry and he pulsed against her once. "Well, I was absolutely sure I could give you a nice juicy orgasm and wait until tomorrow for mine."

Miranda smiled, clasping him close to her, reveling in the feeling of his skin against hers, his naked legs entwined with hers, their bare arms tangled. "Better."

"I love your hair," he said, toying with a long lock of it.

"I love your kissing."

"I love your breasts." He nuzzled her neck and then—groaning—rolled from her. They lay side by side, facing each other. The last of the day's sunlight cascaded into the room. The breeze that lifted the curtains blew over their bodies, and Miranda shivered slightly, as much from reaction as cold.

"Let's get under the covers."

James pulled back the quilt. "Absolutely."

"So, will this ruin your chances to win the race tomorrow?"

"No," he said, and smiled. "Not ruin them. It would have added energy to want to have you and not do it."

"I see," Miranda said lightly. "You were using me."

"Yes, you've found me out."

She drew circles on his brown chest, touching the dark nipples, the scatters of hair between. "It's weird that there is no patron saint of running."

"Well, there is St. Sebastian, the patron saint of athletes."

"But there should be a running saint."

"You should make an altar. It would sell zillions."

"I wonder what she would look like?" The butterflies around the Lady of Mariposa flitted through her imagination. Maybe she would use butterflies, the eternal symbol of transformation. "What is holy about running?"

James closed his eyes, his hand resting easily against her hip. "The wind, the quieting of your mind. The feeling of heat in your limbs."

"The competition?"

His lips turned downward. "Maybe. Swiftness. To be the fastest is pretty exhilarating."

"Should I go home and leave you alone?"

"No, no!" He scooped her close. "Not yet."

Miranda inhaled the scent of his skin, that faint tang of sweat. "I'll be there at the finish line tomorrow. I have to cheer on my dad, too."

He propped himself up on the pillows and looked down at her. "Your dad doesn't seem that bad. He's codependent, but I expected worse, honestly."

"They're probably not that bad apart," Miranda said. "They just made each other miserable for years, and since I was the last one at home…I had a front-row seat."

He curled a finger around hers. "And you're still mad."

"They almost divorced when I was in high school. It went on for ages—a year, maybe two? Fighting and these petty little wars. One would start drinking and carousing and the other one would get furious and take revenge, and yet, there they were, everybody's darling, the scientist and the poet, and their great love story." She rolled her eyes. "They were so caught up in their own story that they forgot they made it up—they just kept acting out these roles, ad infinitum."

"Your father is a stunning writer, Miranda. You must know that."

"Of course I do." She looked at him and waited for the inevitable next words, a pain burning in her chest.

"And you obviously take after him, a creative artist."

Sharply she said, "Oh, yeah, Daddy's girl."

He was quiet for a minute. "I can't guess the story, Miranda. You have to tell me. Or not, of course, but I don't want to guess."

"I'm not his child," she said, and to her horror, tears sprung to her eyes. "I was always Daddy's girl, the apple of his eye, the one everyone said was just like him, and it turns out I'm not even his genetic daughter."

James picked up her hand and kissed the knuckles. "I'm so sorry."

"I hate that they had affairs, that they were so unfaithful to each other, and that I have to keep this bloody secret for everybody else."

"Why do you have to keep it?"

"Oh, because it's so icky. And it's embarrassing and it will freak everyone out."

"It's not all that weird, Miranda. No offense, but it's not even shocking in this world."

She bowed her head. "Maybe I don't want anyone to know. Maybe, for all that he's a pain in the ass, I like being Paul Rousseau's talented daughter."

He didn't say anything, just scooted close and took her into his arms, letting her put her head on his shoulder. He stroked her hair. "That's a pretty good reason."

"Except that it's a lie. Maybe because they lied so much, I just hate lies. And I hate that there is so much of me that belongs to him, and yet it doesn't."

"Like what?"

"My art for one thing. All those altars, because he was so Catholic, because he is so creative."

"A father is more than genetic material."

"I know."

A long silence fell. James threaded his fingers through her hair, and Miranda simply rested against him, reveling in the fit of their bodies, their height and size so perfect together.

She felt him take a breath. "Miranda, I think we need to talk about the reason I left the seminary."

Chapter 13

"Only if you want to tell me."

He wished he didn't have to. Wished it was something dark and dramatic and full of angst, that it wasn't all about lying, even if the lies had not been his own, exactly. "It's important."

"I would like to hear the story of how you went there in the first place, if you wouldn't mind." She raised an eyebrow. "Because I gotta say, *señor*, you seem a bit too lusty to be a priest." She leaned forward and kissed his chest.

"We can start there," he agreed. "When my brother-in-law committed suicide, the person who seemed to offer the most help and practical advice was the priest. We became friends, and I liked what I saw of his work.

He helped people, served the community in a way that seemed hands-on to me. I was sixteen, you know, a little slow to mature, and I was filled with all these passions about changing the world."

Miranda smiled at him, her eyes shining. "I like imagining you at that age, beardless and skinny."

He smiled. "I was a good student and graduated early and chose the seminary before I knew any women. It seemed that I wouldn't miss what I didn't have."

She nodded. "Did you like it?"

"I did. Then a few years later there was a series of ritualistic murders in our community. Gruesome, torture and rape." He cleared his throat. "I knew one of the girls—Sarita—and I took it very hard. It seemed to me that a God who allowed that to happen was not a God I wanted to worship."

"Pretty heavy stuff, I would think, even if you were a very experienced priest."

He nodded.

"But if that's your reason for leaving, it seems like a normal reaction."

"It was the start, but I was actually kicked out for sleeping with one of the women connected to the case. One of the mothers."

Miranda's expression showed a slight, hastily hidden reaction. "One of the mothers? How old was she?"

"Not that old, really. She wasn't quite forty. I was almost twenty." He cleared his throat. "She was grieving, so distraught, and I put my arms around her and tried to comfort her, and she kissed me. I had not ever been kissed before, and it was—well, overwhelming. We started an affair."

Miranda frowned. "If the sex roles were reversed, you'd look like a victim. She took advantage of your youth."

"Perhaps. But youth or not, it was my obligation to be a mentor to her, not lover." He cleared his throat. "Her husband found out, and I was kicked out."

"Her *husband*," Miranda echoed. "Did you know she was married?"

"Not at first. I did later."

She didn't speak for a long moment, then she shifted, covering her breasts with the sheet as she sat up. "I think I need to think about this."

A lump settled in the middle of his chest. "Okay."

Her eyes were troubled. "I appreciate your honesty, James, so I'll give you mine. As deeply attracted to you as I am, the fact that you participated in a relationship like that bothers me."

He touched her arm, not trying to influence her one way or the other. "Take your time. We can talk—"

Her cell phone rang, and Miranda scowled. "Who could be calling me? Okay, it's Juliet."

In the same moment, James's phone rang, too. "Uh-oh."

James found his first. "Hello?"

"James, this is Tam Neville. They found Renate Franz dead just a little while ago."

Miranda was obviously hearing the same news. Her eyes widened. "I'll be right there."

* * *

Miranda felt shaky and disoriented as they rushed to The Black Crown, where Juliet and Josh had assembled to meet Tam and hear the details. It was as if the two extreme functions of her emotions—joy and sorrow—were sticking, and there wasn't much in between. Amid the two extremes was an emotion the muddy-green of a tank: guilt.

What if it was something she'd done that had led to Renate's death?

James said little as they washed up and dressed and headed out. She felt stiff with him for the first time, unsure how to proceed or what her next steps should be.

And yet—good grief!—what a connection! The physical chemistry between them was absolutely perfect. And if she thought about his habit of showing her beautiful things, knowing she would find inspiration in them, she would have said the mental or simpatico connection was very high, too.

But a priest, even a young novice or whatever they were called, who had sex with a grieving mother and a *married* one at that—definitely on the dubious character side of the line.

And what she wanted in a man these days was good character. The thought stunned her, but when she probed it for truth, it stood against her, nudging steadily. A good man of good character, someone responsible and adult and willing to take responsibility for his actions and not do things that would bring drama or trauma or trouble into other people's lives, either.

As they ducked into the bar, Miranda spotted a camera crew talking to Tam, and Juliet had combed her hair and put on lipstick. Josh stood beside her looking thunderous.

"What happened?" Miranda asked.

"Someone killed her with a bullet to the heart and dumped her body in the alley."

"I don't suppose they know who did it," James said.

"No."

Miranda narrowed her eyes. "She got too close to something. I talked to her this morning. Here." Her stomach felt distinctly ill. "It's terrible. She was surprisingly kind to me."

"What time was that?"

"I don't know—just before lunch. Maybe eleven? Max introduced me."

"The police might need to talk to you, Mirrie." Juliet pulled out her cell phone. "It looks better if we volunteer information."

"Sure."

The police took Miranda's information, asked about Max. They also took James's statement about meeting with Elsa this morning.

James and Tam conferred for a long time as Miranda spoke to the police, and when he came back, he took Miranda aside. "Tam is going to leak Desi's plans to sell the land to the Mariposa Utes," he said with a half grin that made her heart flip.

Miranda laughed. "Okay. Has she spoken to them?"

"Josh arranged for the chief of the tribe to come in and talk to Desi this evening. They were more than happy to make the deal, especially since she's been so cooperative with the nation in the past."

"Good. At least that takes some pressure off."

"And now that Renate has been murdered, it looks like a bigger plot around Claude, too, so maybe they'll find some more reasonable suspects for his murder."

"Okay," she said. Then silence. The mannered awkwardness slipped between them again. James said, "Well, I need to get some sleep if I'm going to run my best."

"Okay." Their eyes met and for a long, hip-weakening moment, Miranda's memory was awash with all the things their bodies had enjoyed together, all the pleasure they'd given and received, the heady kisses and explosive joining. Mindful of the others around them, they didn't kiss. James squeezed her hand. "See you tomorrow."

She nodded.

His spine was ever so slightly stiff as he left, and she wondered, with a squeeze of her heart, if she was overreacting to his bombshell. Maybe she was. Maybe she wasn't. Maybe, though, she didn't have to decide this very minute.

As he slipped out into the night, she found herself on her feet and dashing after him. "James," she cried after him as she hit the street.

He turned and she ran up to him in the gloaming to plant a big kiss on his beautiful mouth. "Thank you for such a great day."

He hugged her, silently and closely, then let her go with a kiss to her forehead. "Thank you."

"I will be at the finish line."

"Good."

Juliet went back to her own house after all, perhaps sensing Miranda's high level of discomfort. "Are you okay?" she asked as they dropped their purses on the hallway table.

"It's just sickening that she died. I talked to her today, and now she's dead."

"It's not your fault, Miranda."

"I know." She dropped onto the couch and put her head in her hands, feeling bone-deep weariness in her neck. Flashes of the day moved through her imagination—Renate and Desi and the saris and James, kissing her right here in this house, not five feet from where she sat, and Carol at dinner. "What are we going to do about Mother, Juliet? She can't be allowed to ruin your wedding."

"I talked it over with Josh on the way to the pub. If she wants to come, she has to agree to leave the alcohol alone. She's sometimes astringent when she's sober, but it's the alcohol that makes her evil."

"Agreed." Miranda felt some of the tension drain out of her neck. "Daddy seems very well, in comparison."

"He does. He always is a lot better. I'm never sure why you're so hard on him."

Miranda shrugged.

"Are you aware that you have a giant hicky on your shoulder?"

"What?" Miranda straightened, covering her shoulders with her palms. "Where?"

"Left side." Juliet grinned. "James, I hope."

"Yes." She covered her face. "I'm so embarrassed. Do you think anyone else saw it?"

Laughing, Juliet said, "Who would care, Mirrie? He's a cool guy. I like him a lot for you—he's so calm. And he looks at you like you hung the moon. No kidding."

"Really?" She touched her tummy. "I can't really talk yet. It's too new."

"That's okay. Are you going to be all right now? I've gotta get some sleep."

"I'm fine. The first runners shouldn't finish until about noon, so I'm headed down there a little before, just in case. I told Daddy and James I'd be there."

"All right." Juliet yawned, hugely. "I can't believe I'm getting married in a week! One more week!"

"I'm so happy for you." The wedding talk made her think of the saris, and that made her remember Desi's request.

"Dang it!" she cried. "Desi asked me to go get a blanket for Crazy Horse. He's very upset without it. I promised I'd go get it." She looked at her watch, stunned to see that it was only a little before nine. "If I run up there, I can get back home in an hour."

"You don't like driving at night. I'll do it."

"No way. I'm fine." She stood up, pulling the keys for her rental car out of her purse, and sliding her shoes back out from under the couch. "You get some sleep, and I'll take care of this little errand."

Juliet nodded. "You know what? I'm going to let you. If it were anything else, I'd say it would be okay, but that dog is just plain weird about that blanket, and he'll whine about it all night long. But—" her face brightened and she reached for a bowl on the coffee table that held keys "—take Desi's truck. It's a lot higher and it drives like a dream on those roads."

Miranda grinned. "Cool."

"You remember how to get there?"

"'Course. I was just there yesterday."

It was, Miranda had to admit, a little bit creepy to drive on those very, very dark empty roads. The trees seemed to loom over her and the darkness seemed like a living presence, lurking just beyond the bright circle of headlights. Twice, she saw animals bounding away and prayed she wouldn't inadvertently hit something— but mainly because it would be absolutely terrifying to have to get out of the truck.

Her fear irked her. As a child, she'd been an intrepid outdoors girl. She'd loved coming to Mariposa for summer camp, loved the chance to be by herself in the forest, looking at a mountain or sitting by a creek. It was only the years of living in the noisy, brightly lit city that had chipped away her bravery.

And honestly, there was danger in the mountains— from weather and maybe bears and big cats and getting lost—but the dangers were much more clear and reliable than those a person faced in the city. When she arrived at Desi's cabin, she turned off the engine and the lights and got out of the truck.

There were no lights on in the cabin. The city of Mariposa was far below in the valley, hidden by the forest. Even the glow of lights from the town was rubbed out, leaving behind only starlight to glow over the furry, treeful darkness.

She raised her gaze to those stars—billions and billions of them, glittering, winking, glowing. Blazing planets and tiny, sugarlike scatters of stars, unimaginably distant.

So *many* stars.

Around her the hush of the forest, too, seemed a miracle. A soft whoosh of wind wound through the treetops. A branch creaked. She could hear the ticking of the truck engine, and far away, a wolf howled at the sanctuary, and an animal bolted through the forest, cracking branches. Miranda jumped, but the sound was small, as if a rabbit bolted down a hole.

She raised her eyes again to the sky, that endless, extraordinary sky. It made her life and fears seem very small. She thought of her sisters, and her parents, and of James.

James.

The truth was, she wasn't particularly bothered by his youthful, indiscreet affair. The divine, it was said, moved in mysterious ways, and that was not a man who should *ever* have thought of the priesthood.

She was, however, bothered by her reaction to him. She hardly had known him a week and it was as if he'd filled up a thousand little yawning holes in her, as if something in her had taken one look at him and said, "Finally."

Love at first sight was not real, though.

Was it?

And what if she gave him her heart and it turned out to be one more of her missteps? What if she made a fool of herself and he didn't really love her in return? What if she—

Something cracked in the forest, and Miranda jumped. Stop mooning around, she told herself. She could think about James later. For now, a dog needed his blanket, and it was her job to take care of it.

Her job. As she scurried toward the cabin, laughing at herself for her nervousness, it occurred to her that she was feeling a lot of pride in becoming a member of the tribe that held her sisters and their husbands. It felt good to have a place, if she wanted it. For the first time in her life, she really felt like she did belong. Here, amid the art community in Mariposa. Here with her sisters and their families. Here where she would have a chance to spoil nieces and nephews. Here where she might, in the peace and quiet, discover where her art would next take her.

As she unlocked the front door, the wolves howled again, and Miranda was sure she heard a rustling in the trees. Urgently she shoved open the door to the cabin and slammed it behind her, still laughing at her own silly nervousness. She found a light switch and flipped it to turn it on. Nothing happened, but there was enough starlight—who knew it would illuminate so well?—

that she could make her way to the little lamp near the door, and turned that on. It gave a small, yellow pool of light into the world, and Miranda spied the blanket, right where she remembered it.

She picked it up and looked around. The rooms smelled a little stale, almost like mothballs or something like that. She inhaled, trying to identify the scent, but gave up. Probably just musty from being closed up in the heat the past few days, or maybe it was some ointment Desi used on the dogs.

Was there anything else Desi might want while she was here? She reached for her phone and realized her purse was in the car. Oh, well.

Feeling good about herself and her ability to do what other people needed her to do, she turned off the light, headed outside and made sure the door was locked behind her. She stepped off the porch and was nearly to the truck when the explosion knocked her down.

Chapter 14

Her body flew forward, and she crashed into the ground, but the blanket cushioned the landing. Stunned, she didn't move for a moment, hearing a roar behind her.

The smell of wood burning yanked her from the shock of the landing. Scrambling to her feet, she whirled around and saw that the cabin was on fire.

"Oh, my God!" She flew to the door of the truck and threw the blanket inside, scrambling in her purse for the phone. With shaking fingers, she punched in 911, and waited, but the call didn't go through. She tried it again.

Flames licked at the back of the house, but Miranda could see the fire was not very well established. Something had blown up—maybe a propane tank or something?—but it was only at the front of the house right this minute. Bringing the phone with her to repeat the phone call, she rushed around to the kitchen side of the house, where a small garden water pump stood near the back porch. She scrambled for something to put water in, and could see nothing.

The front of the house was on fire, but not the back. She took a calculated risk and kicked open the back door. Smoke billowed out, and she had a bewildered moment of trying to figure out how something blew up at the front door when the propane tanks were in the side yard, but there wasn't time for trying to sort it out this minute. Coughing, she covered her face with a scarf by the door and flung open the cupboards, looking for a fire extinguisher or a big pot to put the water in. In a moment of inspiration, she plugged the kitchen sink and turned on the water full force, then ran to the bathroom and did the same thing, turning on the shower, too, and racing back out.

Back outside, she started filling a kitchen pot with water, then saw a hose coiled up neatly beneath the kitchen window, and chortled happily. She attached it to the pump, which was hooked to the reservoir, and flung open the nozzle and headed around the house, breathing hard, her eyes stinging with smoke. She redialed the number, and it rang once, but she lost the signal.

"Damn!" she cried.

The hose wouldn't reach this way. It shot water just short of the burning front door. She dragged it to the kitchen door, and with some regret for the water damage, shot the stream right at the front door. Steam and smoke billowed out from the spot, but in a minute, it did seem to be working.

Her eyes streamed with irritation. She ducked her face into the crook of her left arm, holding the hose with the right. Steam and the sound of water spitting against heat comforted her. She'd get most of it out and then head down the mountain and get some help, though sooner or later she was bound to get through to 911.

She punched the redial button, and there was a long pause, then a mechanical voice said, "Connection lost. Redialing."

The smoke and the sound of the fire were getting more intense, and Miranda couldn't see very well. She kept the phone to her ear, coughing, her eyes streaming.

When something slammed into her from the side, she screamed, thinking at first that it was a part of the roof falling down to trap her. She reared back, the hose flying out of her hands to soak the air, soak her head and shoulders. The edge of it slammed into her forehead, and a hard shot of water filled her nose and mouth. She gagged. The phone went flying.

Only then did she realize that it was a body that had knocked her down, a body with hands that reached for her neck. Blinded, Miranda flung an arm up, connecting with something she thought might be ribs, which gave her time to scramble away. A hand grabbed her ankle and Miranda kicked backward, urgently wiping at her eyes, coughing hard in the smoke. The body landed on her, hard, smashing her against the floor, and Miranda's hands landed on something burning hot. With a howl, she pulled away, scooting in the other direction, aware of hands trying to hold her, a body attempting to weigh her down.

A part of her screamed, *this is not fair!* She slammed her arms into the body, wished she could see, kept her body in motion, trying to imagine herself as slippery as an eel.

The body grabbed her hair and yanked hard, and Miranda's neck jerked backward painfully, and then there were hands around her throat, squeezing. She couldn't breathe, couldn't seem to shift her body to get free, and the more she struggled, the more she struggled for air.

Time shifted. She saw flashes of Desi, and her own awkwardness in hugging her even when she was hurt. There was a flash of Juliet's wedding, conspicuously empty without her. She saw her father trying to make conversation with her, and smooth things over with their mother, and generally, always, trying.

And she saw James. So good and clear and honorable, so handsome and good to her. They had had a chance to make something real and lasting and Miranda had run away in pride.

Pride.

Always her stiff-necked pride, getting in her way.

The edges of her vision started to blacken and every

cell in her body screamed for oxygen and there was fire licking at the soles of her feet. The body on top of her was heavy, crushing.

The horrifying truth came home. She would die if she didn't win this struggle. Die!

Hands burning, eyes streaming, lungs bursting, she focused everything she had to knock the body off of her. She tried to kick, but her oxygen was depleting and she didn't have much strength left. She opened her eyes, hoping to have a chance to make a connection, but the light was murky, red. Everything was on fire now, all around them, things popping and burning and the big, heavy figure over her.

And suddenly she remembered the rules of a self-defense class she'd taken at Juliet's insistence. When faced with a stranglehold, go limp, then lift the arms between the attackers, and break the hold by flinging your arms outward.

She went limp, not as easy as one would imagine under the circumstances.

Her attacker eased his hold slightly.

Miranda swiftly lifted her arms between his, flung them outward. Her rigid arms slammed into his elbows and they buckled, then she was abruptly free. Gagging, coughing, sucking in air, she rolled sideways, and scrambled away as fast as she could, sliding and splashing on the water that pooled on the floor. She realized she could see, maybe because her tears had cleared her vision, or perhaps the smoke had shifted.

Whatever. Hearing her attacker come behind, she

rushed to find anything that could be used as a weapon and grabbed the only thing at hand—the hose. She swung it, the water pouring out, and smacked him with the hard end. He staggered, and the water hit him full in the face, and he skittered backward, slamming into the post of the front door that was on fire. In a flash, his sleeve was afire, and he screamed, trying to shed it as fast as he could, but his body weight, slamming into that burning post, knocked the loosened threshold down and he was trapped. He screamed as another fiery beam fell, and then he was silent.

For a long minute, she leaned on the porch step on her hands and knees, water pouring out of the hose to make a puddle at her feet. Her throat burned and her lungs felt as if they'd been turned inside out, and she heaved suddenly, choking on smoke and terror and injury.

She fell in the cool grass, body exhausted, and stared up at the sky full of stars, aware that the fire was out of control, that she needed to get up and see if she could find the phone, or get back in the truck and get down the mountain, but she couldn't move. Not one muscle.

Far in the distance, she heard sirens. And that was the last she heard for a good long while.

When she did surface, it was to the unpleasant sensation of a cold liquid entering her veins through her left arm. She startled, rearing up ready to fight, disoriented by time, terror, location. Arms captured her, around the shoulders and at her head. "You're safe," a woman's voice said in a soothing tone. "Honey, you're safe. He's dead."

Miranda sucked in a big gasp of air and coughed, the sound deep and ragged. She felt like she'd cough up her guts. The woman made soothing noises. "It's okay, it's all right."

Blinking at the light overhead, Miranda tried to talk and found she couldn't utter a word. It was as if her throat had been scrubbed free of a voice box. She put a hand to her throat and tried to find the woman who was speaking.

Her face came into view, a kind, youngish face with red cheeks and curly black hair. "Don't try to talk. Between the smoke inhalation and the strangling, your voice is going to be a little raw for a few days."

Miranda peered at the surroundings. She widened her eyes in a question.

"You're in an ambulance. We're transporting you to the community hospital. You have burns on your hands and arms and some pretty serious bruising on your throat."

Now Miranda could feel her palms. Stinging in a deep and highly unpleasant way. She wanted to raise them to look at them, but the woman shook her head. "Let's let them fix them up a bit first."

She nodded. She wanted to ask a thousand questions—where was the guy who tried to kill her? Was the house a loss?

Suddenly, she remembered the blanket. In a ragged, ragged voice with barely any sound, she said, "Blanket in the back of the truck for a dog. Need it." The words scratched her throat like nails. "Important."

"Okay. I'll have somebody fetch it. The truck is fine."

Miranda raised her eyebrows. House? she whispered, but it was barely audible and the woman didn't seem to hear.

Juliet was at the hospital emergency room when Miranda arrived, and sat with Miranda as she was examined, head to toe. Miraculously, aside from some smoke inhalation, the bruised throat and badly burned palms, she was not injured.

A firefighter brought the blanket in just as they were getting ready to go. "Here you go," he said. "It's a little damp, but not otherwise messed up."

Miranda bowed her thanks, putting gauze-wrapped hands together in a prayer position. "Man?" she mouthed, point at her throat.

"Dead. We don't know who he is but we'll find out."

Communication was difficult, between the bandaged palms and sore throat. "House?" she croaked out.

"Gone," he said. "I'm sorry."

They drove back in silence, taking two minutes to go by Helene's house to drop off the blanket. Juliet said, coming back to the truck, "He curled up right on it, so happily."

She nodded.

Juliet drove them home. "He almost killed you, honey," she said. "I am so sorry I didn't go."

Fiercely, and without hesitation, Miranda hugged her sister. "No," she whispered. "I'm okay."

"I'll let you sleep in tomorrow morning."

Again Miranda was fierce. *No.* There was a lot that had become clear to her as she'd struggled in that smoky world. Nearly all of it could be addressed by going to that race tomorrow.

Hell or high water.

James rose at five and showered as was his ritual. He put on his favorite running shorts and singlet, and wrist bands. Barefoot, he drank a cup of coffee and ate half a bagel smeared with peanut butter, then sat out on the balcony and recited the whole of the rosary, methodically clearing everything out of his mind but the coming race. When that was finished, he ate the other half of his bagel, filled a plastic bottle with water, another with energy gel and put them in their special belt, then put on his shoes and went down to the race registration, a big tent just off the main drag.

He loved the somehow hushed, focused spirit that gathered in the air on race starts. Runners stretched and jogged loosely and did quick sprints. They wore jogging pants and sweats, T-shirts and running bras and singlets like his own. This was a mountain run, so there were more than the usual number of eccentrics— a man with a beard to his waist running without shoes or shirt, but gloves on his hands, an old woman in neon-orange who'd probably kick a good bit of butt by the look of her rangy legs, a good cross-section of adventure racers who trained in the mountains.

James didn't talk to anyone. He didn't see anyone

he knew, either, which wasn't surprising. He got his number and pinned it on, then stretched a little and just jogged very slowly around the perimeter, turning his focus back to himself. To the race.

The sun was just coming up as the gun went off and the racers surged toward the trail, running in a thick pack down Black Diamond Boulevard to the first of the big climbs, the first one to sort the men from the boys, as it were. James let himself flow into it, focusing on keeping his pace absolutely steady, knowing within an hour who he'd be fighting for the finish. He kept running, smooth and steady. Sometimes in the lead, sometimes running in a small knot. At mile eleven, they lost a young turk who pushed too hard over the rocky ridge. James passed him, limping along with ragged breathing. He'd hit the wall.

James kept running.

To Miranda, waiting at the end.

The newspapers were full of Renate's murder the next morning. Miranda woke up feeling stiff and without much energy, but she was absolutely determined not to be kept from her appointment, especially because her cell phone was gone—lost to the fire.

She showered, careful to keep her bandaged hands dry, and dressed equally carefully in a pretty skirt and top. In the mirror, she looked a little tired, but not terrible. Her hair had scorched a little at the ends, but the dousing with the hose had saved it. Her face was a little bruised along her chin, but not noticeably.

Her throat, on the other hand, looked shockingly bad. Enough that it would make people uncomfortable to look at her. She dug through her suitcase and found a soft, long scarf knitted out of a metallic shimmer lace. She looped it twice around her throat, loosely, and it covered it fine.

Juliet was waiting in the kitchen. "Good morning, brave girl. Can you talk yet?"

"I can whisper, but even that hurts a little."

"Okay, here's the deal. I've been on the phone with the sheriff and it appears that the house was rigged to blow when the light switch was flipped. Luckily it didn't quite go off the way it was supposed to, so you got lucky."

"Who is it?"

"He has a record for theft and arson, but they haven't tracked it all down yet."

Miranda nodded. "Does Desi know?"

"Oh, yeah, and she is fit to be tied." She grinned. "At this very moment, she's meeting with the Ute tribal council, to see if they want to make a bid on the land."

With a grin, Miranda pumped the air. "Brilliant," she whispered. She glanced at the clock, and pointed. "I'm going to ReNew for some chai. See you later?"

"Absolutely."

Miranda bought the newspapers in front of ReNew, which was insanely crowded with relatives and friends of the runners. A part of her wanted to be annoyed with them, taking up space in *her* restaurant, but why was it any more hers than theirs? She squeezed into a corner with her chai and cinnamon twist to read about Renate Franz's murder.

Even the Denver papers carried the story, laden as it was with big-name Olympic sports and layerings of the art world, and speculations about business. In a sidebar in the Denver Post, there was a photo of Desi and Tam from an earlier news story, along with news of the fire.

She grinned to herself over Desi's move to sell the land to the Utes. So smart! It benefited the tribe in ways the casinos never could, something that was important to Desi, and the tribe would likely take care of the land more responsibly. And it would mean Desi would finally be out of danger.

Although not yet cleared. The newspaper still called Desi "a person of interest in the murder of her husband, Navajo artist Claude Tsosie."

According to the article, the police didn't have any leads in the shooting of Franz. But suddenly, Miranda wondered how Elsa was taking it. Might be worth finding out.

It would be even better if the whole thing just died a natural death. If Desi were let off the hook, the land went to the Utes, and whoever killed Claude fell over a mountain somewhere.

And they could all just live happily ever after.

She certainly intended to. The air this morning seemed freshly washed, sparkling with possibilities. She felt she'd been given a reprieve, a chance to throw off the shackles of her control and cynicism and live a freer, fuller life. In memory, she kept seeing the expanse of that bejeweled sky, the distance and hugeness, and her sense of her own small importance in it.

And yet, each star sparkled, each one added its own light. She would do what she could to make sure she added hers instead of hiding it.

After she finished her coffee, she headed over to the race tent. The day was painted in blues—blue sky, blue mountains, blue and white tent. A small crowd milled around, looking at the jewelry and paintings offered by the booths set up to take advantage of the people drawn by the race. Miranda drifted by them, admiring blown glass beads and intricately laced ribbon bracelets, and the omnipresent flower crowns woven with ribbons that seemed to show up at festivals everywhere. Miranda thought of Glory and her very long hair, and bought one made of tiny rose pink rosebuds. "Will this fit a five-year-old?" she asked in her ruined voice.

"It will." The woman, well into her sixties, with sun-worn skin and irregular teeth, said, "You need one for yourself, dear. All that hair."

Miranda smiled, shaking her head.

The woman held up one woven of vivid blue bachelor buttons and sprays of white baby's breath. It was almost the exact color of her sari, and impulsively, she thought, why not. "Okay," she whispered, and paid for them both. Glory's went into a little bag. Her own went on her hair. On her hair, her beautiful hair, which had almost been burned off. She would never apologize for it again.

She looked at her watch. Not quite ten. The first runners wouldn't be back until just after eleven, probably. She really needed to be here when James came down that mountain. Restlessly she walked circles around the block, thinking.

Renate, Christie, Elsa, Claude. The land. Claude's paintings. Somehow it was all connected, she could feel it.

As she came around the corner the third time, she saw her mother sitting on a bench, a white hat shading her face. Dressed crisply in white capris and a turquoise top and white shoes, she looked ready for a day on a boat. Her lipstick was coral. She'd brought a magazine with her.

Miranda froze. Did she go sit with her mother or keep walking around the block?

As if someone shoved her from behind, Miranda took a stumbling step forward. Fine. She'd go sit with her mother. Tossing back her hair, she hoped her hicky showed.

"Good morning, Mother," she said, taking the seat next to her.

"Hello, Miranda." Her mother gave her a quizzical glance. "What's wrong with your voice? And your hands?"

"Long story."

"Hmm. Your hair looks pretty like that."

Surprised, Miranda said, "Thanks."

"Did you see your young man off this morning?"

"He's not really my young man, but no way. I think the race started at six-thirty or seven."

"He seems a nice fellow. You and your sisters have all gone for such dark men, my goodness! Between Desi and Juliet, we'll have three or four nationalities covered!"

Miranda told herself to just breathe through her annoyance. "Well, that's America for you these days. I bet Desi and Tam will have linebacker children."

"You never know. Look how different you girls all are."

"Mother, please."

"Please what? You are all quite different."

"I have a different father. That might account for some of it, huh?"

"What are you talking about, Miranda?" Back to her mom's old denial routine.

"Mom, I was there, the whole year when you and Daddy were fighting. I heard you tell him I was not his child."

"Oh, that." Carol waved a hand. "Big lie."

"So he *is* my father?"

"In every way that matters."

Miranda gritted her teeth. "So he *isn't?*"

"Let it go, honey." She shaded her eyes with a hand. "Anyway, look at the top of the mountain. There's a runner." Same mother. Same denial routine. Miranda wondered why she continued to even bother. Seeing the runner, she couldn't help but think of more important things…like James.

"Oh, my gosh!" Miranda looked at her watch. It would take a while for that runner to get to the bottom of the trail, but still, the time was going to be a very, very good one. It was a lone runner, out in front. Way out in front, and it was impossible to tell much detail. He wore a white singlet and blue shorts and had dark hair.

She jumped up. "I think it could be James!" Her throat hurt, and she laughed anyway, so excited. "Wow, what if he wins! Wouldn't that be cool?"

"Not your young man, hmm?"

"We haven't known each other but a few days."

"Sometimes, Miranda, you just know. I met your father at a party when I was twenty-three and we've been inseparable ever since."

Miranda bit her tongue. "I know, I've heard the story."

"We love each other, you know. I don't claim to be a perfect person, and God knows you had a bad time of it especially, but the one thing that's true is your father and me."

It was so passionately said that Miranda was shaken into a new look at her mother. "Is everything okay, Mom?"

"It's fine."

But Miranda saw the fine trembling of her mother's lips and knew it wasn't. She didn't push it. For once, she just let things be. She put her arm around her mother and gave her a bracing little hug. "Let's go cheer on the finishers, shall we?"

Carol nodded, looking suddenly every day of her sixty years. "I'm sorry about last night," she said suddenly.

Miranda stared at her. "Apology accepted. Once you get to know Glory, you'll fall in love with her. We all have."

"I'm sure."

A few more runners came around the top of the hill, but the one in front was still in the lead. His pace was steady, absolutely even, his shoulders back, head tall. As they stood there, a butterfly fluttered around her face, a mourning cloak butterfly with black and blue wings. Miranda felt it land on her shoulder, and just let it be, thanking it for the blessing of its presence, feeling absolutely connected to everything holy.

And she could see now that it was clearly James. He ran like a gazelle, as if it required no effort, his legs lifting, moving, lifting, moving, his arms pumping, hands loose.

Miranda had never been much for sports, or athletes, until Max, and that had not happened because of his skiing but in spite of it, on the off-season. She had always held a certain scorn for those who ran or cycled, pouring their passion into something so disciplined and unappealing.

But James, running, was one of the most beautiful sights she'd ever seen. As he ran down the mountain, his face a blank mask of concentration, her heart swelled.

"He is a beautiful runner," her mother said beside her.

Miranda knew the exact moment when James spied her. He still did not break rhythm, just ran steadily, steadily, steadily toward her, his eyes burning. And suddenly, he was running very, very fast. The power surge.

If it wasn't so damned geeky, she would have had tears in her eyes.

An old man waited nearby the ribbon drawn across the finish line, a stopwatch in his hand. A crew of other race coordinators were there, too, cameras and hats and papers in hand. As James crossed the finish, the old man chortled, pumping his fist in the air. "Three hours, thirty-one minutes! New record!"

James slowed to a walk, pacing out, his chest heaving. Sweat coated his chest, back, arms. His hair, slick and black above a red sweatband, was soaked through, and he took two cups of water, pouring one over his head, drinking the other down, still pacing. He raised a hand at Miranda and she, familiar with this part from years of her father's races, waited until he went through his finishing routine. The judges gave him a medal, his picture was taken a dozen times and the crowd was cheering. The old man came over and gave him a hug, and Miranda felt her throat tighten.

"I think that's Peter Bok," Carol said. "He's famous for winning this race for something like twenty years in a row."

"Seventeen," Miranda whispered.

The other racers, a trail of three, then another two, were nearing the last stretch. When they straggled across the finish line, Miranda waited to hear the time: three hours, forty-four minutes. She smiled at James, who was walking toward her, a grin on his angled, exotic face. Before she could say a word, he grabbed her and kissed her, and he smelled of sunlight and good, healthy sweat, and the pheromones in his scent just about knocked her flat. A blistering series of images flashed in her mind as he kissed her, and she didn't pull away, though she giggled at his display. "Eww, ewww, eww!" she said as he let her go. "Man sweat. Cooties."

He laughed and bent, putting his hands on his knees, stretching his lower back, maybe his hamstrings. "That was some race. Everything just flowed. I'm really pumped just this minute."

"Congratulations," she said. "New record. Oooh. That's very sexy."

He peered at her. "What happened to you?"

"Long story. Tell you later."

He reached for the scarf around her neck and she grabbed his hand. Hard. "Leave it alone, James."

His eyes burned. "For now," he agreed.

Carol offered her hand politely. "Well done," she said.

"Thank you." He drank from a bottle of blue sports drink. "Listen, I'm going to go shower and get something to eat. Do you want to wait here, or come with me?"

"I'll stay here and wait to see my dad come through."

"You have time to go and come back before your father finishes, Miranda. He'll be another hour."

"I'll wait with you," she insisted.

James leaned in and gave her another kiss. "Won't take me long and then I need some serious calories, and we can go see what the sheriff has turned up on Renate Franz."

"It's a deal."

He raised a hand and walked off toward the hotel, three blocks away. To her mother Miranda said, "*Look* at those legs."

"Very nice." She raised an eyebrow. "And runners tend to have a lot of stamina, you know. Well into late life."

Miranda clapped her hands over her ears. "Too much information, Mother!" But she was laughing.

Carol's cell phone trilled politely in her handbag. "Oh, dear. Excuse me. Hello?" She listened. "Yes, she's here. One moment, please." She handed the phone to Miranda. "It's Juliet."

"Hello?" Miranda said. "Daddy hasn't come in yet, but James won!"

"That's great," Juliet replied. "Listen, some very interesting DNA information has surfaced, and you might want to go with James to check it out. The deputy just called me."

"Okay." Her voice was starting to hurt. A lot. She cleared her throat, but that made it worse.

"Sorry. Don't talk. It looks like they might drop the charges against Desi, completely."

"Good."

"Come back to the house when you've seen the evidence, and we'll see what's going on."

Chapter 15

Miranda's father made it over the finish line in a respectable 4:50—taking third place in his age group—but not in very good shape. She could tell he was very pleased to see her, and she pumped the air visibly for him, even though her voice wouldn't allow her to cheer. He was gray and dehydrated and they took him to the Red Cross tent for tending. Carol fluttered around him and he growled her away, but allowed her to hold his hand as he took IV fluids.

She found James at the hotel restaurant eating dinner. "Where's your phone?" he asked.

"I have a story to tell you," she croaked, and unwound the scarf to reveal the bruises on her throat. "But I have to use few words, okay?"

His eyes blazed and he put down the fork, and moved close to put his head on her shoulder, and swore. "Who did it?"

"Dead. Desi's cabin burned. We need to go to the police station, you can get the story from them."

So they headed over to the sheriff's department, which was abuzz with reporters and activity. A harassed young woman barked, "Can I help you?" when they approached the desk, but upon finding out who they were, led them back to a desk in the back of the room, where a stout, middle-aged man worked on a pile of papers. What remained of his hair stuck out all over his head, as if he'd had his fingers in it all day, and it made Miranda feel protectively tender. He seemed to know it was a mess, and rubbed a smoothing hand over it. His nameplate read Sergeant Rinehart.

"How are you, Ms. Rousseau?"

She nodded, shrugged, gestured to her throat with widened eyes.

"It hurts," James said. "I'd like to talk for her as much as possible. And I'd like more answers."

"DNA," she said.

"What?" James asked, but the deputy was already shuffling through the papers.

"We'll get to last night in a minute. But first, yeah, there's been an interesting bit of business that surfaced in this case. We ran DNA on the Franz woman, just to see where it stood with the murder, and it turns out she's related to Claude Tsosie."

"What?" Miranda couldn't help herself. "Related how?"

"Siblings, maybe. Very close."

"She has another sister in town," James said. "Elsa Franz. You should run her, too."

"If she cooperated, we could do it, but at the moment, she's not speaking to the press or the police or anyone else. And unless there's some reason to suspect her in the murders, there's no reason to force her."

Poor thing, Miranda thought. But her head buzzed with the implications and possibilities in the fact that Claude and Renate were related. She shook her head.

"Are you going to drop the charges against Desi now?" James asked.

"I don't think she's the killer." He rubbed his forehead. "We're on it."

"Tell me what happened last night."

The sheriff explained the basic details. Miranda had gone to the cabin to pick something up for her sister, who was in the hospital.

"A blanket," she croaked. "For the dog."

James gave her a look she couldn't interpret. "A dog blanket? At ten o'clock at night."

"He can't sleep."

He chuckled. "Okay." To the sheriff he said, "Go on."

"Someone rigged the house to blow when the front light switch was turned on, but there was a delay. As Miranda there was leaving, the explosives blew, knocking the front door out."

James swore softly beneath his breath.

"Miranda," Rinehart said, "correct me if I get any of this wrong."

She nodded.

"It must have knocked you down—"

Another nod.

"—and then she went around to the back, hooked up the hose and turned on the water in the kitchen and bathroom."

"Called 911," she coughed out. "Cut off. Kept calling."

"Right. At some point, it must have gotten through, because the dispatcher heard screams and sounds of a struggle. She used GPS to find the phone, saw that it was Desi's place—she knows her—and sent a paramedic, too.

"By the time they got there, the guy was dead—trapped when a beam fell, and Miranda was passed out from smoke inhalation, outside in the grass."

"You kicked his ass, huh?" James said, taking her bandaged hand gently, and kissing a spot that wasn't bandaged.

"Did my best."

"When you can," the sergeant said, "we need a complete statement from you."

"Who's the perpetrator?" James asked.

"A petty thug from Denver. Haven't been able to make a connection to anybody in particular, but it's pretty obvious somebody hired him."

James nodded. "All right. Is there anything else?"

"Nope. Not from our side."

From behind them came an uproar, the reporters going nuts as someone came inside. Miranda turned, half expecting Desi. Instead she could see the top of a blond head over the tops of the reporters.

"Elsa," she rasped out to James.

A trio came through the doors, all blond and fit and beautiful: Elsa, Christie, and Max. Christie hovered protectively close to Elsa, who was wearing Jackie O sunglasses herself, big, black glasses that hid half her face and still couldn't hide the wanness of her complexion.

The desk clerk heard their comment, then brought them back to the sergeant. Miranda and James exchanged a look.

Max and Christie flanked the very tall, lovely Elsa, who looked shaky and unstable. When Max caught sight of Miranda, he looked visibly shaken, and he paused to give her a Continental greeting and look sympathetically at her bandaged hands. Christie ignored her, and helped settle Elsa in a chair.

"You want to hear this, too," the desk clerk said to Miranda.

"I need to tell the truth," she said, and pulled off her glasses. Her eyes were red from weeping. "About all the things I know that have happened."

"I'm happy to hear whatever you want to tell me, miss. Start with your name, please."

"Elsa Franz Biloxi. My sister was Renate Franz. My brother was Claude Franz, whom you know as Claude Tsosie."

Miranda couldn't help the gasp.

"I knew it," James said with satisfaction.

"My sister killed my brother when he started seeing Christie. Christie was our friend from a long time ago, and Renate told him to leave her alone, because she is a talented athlete and Claude was not good to women. It was the last straw. Claude was greedy and he didn't care about anyone but himself."

Miranda looked at Christie. In this light, the girl looked painfully young, brokenhearted in the way only a young woman can be. She was sure she would never love again.

"Your sister shot him."

"Yes."

"Just because he wouldn't leave Christie alone?"

Elsa sighed. "That was the—how do you say it?— the last thing."

"Last straw," Christie said.

"Yes." She took a breath. "It is so complicated. We all wanted to come to America, become rich. Renate was a painter, and Claude—always so pretty, he was, and we came to the Grand Canyon? When he was a teenager, and he was wearing hair long, part of a rock band, you know? Everyone thought he was Indian."

Miranda felt disoriented. She'd not known her brother-in-law particularly well, but it seemed everything about him was a lie. She wondered how Desi would take it.

Elsa continued, "Renate is very smart, you know? She is the oldest of us, and she thought and thought, and studied, and we went to New York first. I was very young, not yet twelve, and Renate set up her business. She was still painting, and started doing some very good work with the material from our trip to the Grand Canyon, all these native images that really spoke to her. She opened a gallery, to make money."

Miranda the artist ached for Renate the artist, who'd been so used.

"Claude went to Arizona," Elsa continued, "then studied at college and went to Peru, where he met Desi." She gave an apologetic glance to Miranda. "Who was rich."

Miranda nodded.

"And that was that. Claude pretended to be a painter. Renate sold his work in her gallery, and I met Bill, and we were all in the soup. No, the gravy."

A couple of chuckles escaped. Elsa shrugged.

"But Claude couldn't leave women alone. Lots of women, but he was careful for a long time. Then he had an affair with a dentist's wife, and she was a little bit crazy. She didn't like it when he broke it off and moved to Christie, and that was when everything started to fall apart with Desi, and we needed her because of the land."

"Did you know about the aquifer?" the sergeant asked.

"Bill, my husband, had some surveys done for my land, for the spa, and they found the aquifer. The plan was to have Claude talk Desi into a partnership, and then we'd all get even richer from the energy sales. Richer than our wildest dreams."

"But Claude couldn't leave other women alone."

"And Renate was fond of Christie. She believed in her, and didn't want her chances for more gold to be hurt. He'd ruined everything by then—like our father did—and Renate felt it was her obligation, to protect me and her. After having Claude take all of her glory, then ignore her pleas to leave our friend alone. It was too much for her."

Miranda felt unexpectedly moved by the story, and blinked away a tear. "Who killed her?"

"It was a thug, the one who started the fire." She looked down. "There is a coalition to get the land. If Desi is gone, the land would be up for sale and they could get it. But Renate was going to tell everything. The reason she came here this summer was to make sure Desi didn't go to jail. She was furious about Claude getting all the credit for her work, too."

"So they killed her. And when Desi went home, she would have been killed, too."

"Ya." She bent over and began to weep. "She is the only person I had in the world!"

Max and Christie flanked her protectively. James said to Christie, "Did you know?"

Christie shook her head. "No. I know everyone thinks I'm a fool, but I loved him."

James stood up. "I guess we'll go spread the news, huh?"

Miranda paused. She knelt beside the weeping woman and touched her hair. "Thank you," she whispered. "You can be our sister if you like. Because you saved Desi's life." Her own eyes filled with tears. "I'm so sorry for your loss."

And as if Miranda's ruined, raw voice unlocked some terrible box, Elsa broke down entirely. She nodded.

James waited, then took Miranda's elbow and they went out into the bright, sunny day. They stood side by side in silence, letting the sun wash down upon them.

Three days later, three sisters put on their hiking boots and carried their offerings up the hill. They had various broken parts among them—Miranda's voice, and Desi's broken arm and Juliet's lingering night-mares, but they carried candles and flowers up the hill to the Shrine of Our Lady of Butterflies for another reason.

It was Miranda's idea. The long moments in Desi's cabin when she thought she would die had shattered the cocoon of cynicism she'd protectively built, and she saw that her family—imperfect, even terribly flawed—was still a family, and they needed to let go of the wounds of childhood to take the mantle of their new lives.

The story of the Shrine had been repeated to Miranda several times. A young girl, born with club feet had promised to make a trek to a waterfall the Indians had held as sacred, one that fell into a rich mineral spring known to have healing properties. It took her three days to make the pilgrimage, but when she arrived, a thousand butterflies had touched her all over and her feet were transformed.

Miranda also knew the science of the place. The waterfall was a cold mountain stream, fed by snowmelt. It fell into a wide, hot pond fed by a vigorous hot spring known to be exceedingly rich in healing minerals. The steam created by the meeting warmed the meadow and provided a haven for butterflies. Not so miraculous, all in all.

Shrines, in general, she'd found, were not. They were pretty. They had nice feelings attached to them. They cheered people and helped them to heal themselves, and there was nothing wrong with that.

The trail to the meadow was deserted, oddly enough, and they found themselves arriving at the grotto alone. Miranda felt a fluttering of excitement as they ducked between the sheltering arms of pines and turned into an open meadow.

"Oh!" she gasped.

It was beyond beautiful. The meadow butted up against a wall of red rock that encircled it like a bowl. High above, trees grew, and down the cliff were vigorous shrubs and clumps of wildflowers, blue and white and yellow and orange, all vibrantly blooming in tumble. The green grassy meadow was dotted with flowers, too, and tall trees grew almost as a roof for the shallow pond, into which a sparkling clear waterfall tumbled, falling from the top of the red wall. Steam hissed quietly from the surface of the pond. A carving of Notre Dame de Mariposa, dark and lovely, was covered with butterflies. The usual mourning cloak, but also yellow and white and purple ones, small and large, fancy and plain.

Miranda could barely breathe with the beauty of it. Awed, her breath a faraway and forgotten thing, she moved into the meadow.

Thousands and thousands of butterflies stirred as they came into the meadow, their wings flashing in the sunlight, swirling around them in soft washes, touching their faces and hands and legs. Miranda laughed. "Butterfly kisses!" she cried, and held out her arms, letting them land all over her, tipping her face back to let them sweep their wings over her face, her throat.

She had been to dozens of shrines, here and in Europe, and never had she felt one so right. It had a holy feeling to it, and to honor that, she said, "Thank you. I'm ready now for whatever you have for me."

The three sisters then lit candles. Juliet went first, and the other two left her to offer her petitions, thanks, prayers by herself. She was there a long while. She returned, beaming, tossing her lion mane of hair away from her face.

Next went Desi, strong and hearty and loyal as a wolf. Her prayers were simple and straightforward, and she returned in only a moment. "If these things are to be trusted, I'm going to have a boy."

"Hooray!" Juliet said.

Miranda went last. She didn't know what to ask for as she knelt in the grass, smelling minerals and freshness from the water, the butterflies dancing around her head. "I've wandered the world," she said to the kindly beneficent face. "I haven't wanted to believe in anything. Now, I think I might have found my man, but I'm too afraid of pain and rejection to love him. I don't know where to live, what to do for my art, how to proceed—but here I am, earnestly listening."

She bowed her head and waited for a picture, or a nudging, or an idea to come to her. None did.

She said the things they'd agreed to say about their family, adding her petition to theirs, then stood and turned around.

And there, looking slightly flummoxed, was James. Her sisters were at the edge of the meadow, waiting. "Do you want us to wait?"

She frowned a little, wondering if they'd done this on purpose. But she waved them on. They turned and headed out of the meadow, back to Mariposa.

"Hello," Miranda said. "What brings you here?"

"Um. I saw you head this way." He swallowed. "Why are you here?"

He looked like a saint or a priest, his dark hair so shiny and thick, his face earnest and real. Butterflies danced around him in the shape of a halo, and Miranda thought that was a bit over the top, but okay. "To pray for my family."

"Only your family?"

"No. For me, too." She smiled. "For direction."

"You should see yourself," he said. "Butterflies are almost touching you all over, so you have, like, a halo."

In the air was musical laughter, and Miranda looked around herself to see it was true. She had a halo, too. "What happens, do you think, if we kiss here?"

He moved forward, and the butterflies came with

him, and came with her. They met, hands outstretched, and when they joined hands, a bright electric shock when their palms touched. "Ow!" she said, but he didn't let go.

He tucked her close, bent his head and kissed her. His body was wiry and hard next to her softness, his lips full as a song, his heart pounding so loud she could hear it, in time with her own. "I love you," he said. "I know it's fast, but I don't care. I love you. I want to be with you."

"It was love at first sight for me, James. Just like that. I saw you and I knew you were my man. My soul mate."

"I thought you didn't believe in soul mates."

"I didn't until I met mine." She smiled up at him. "Oh, I am so sorry for being a fool."

"I've been too prideful. I'm sorry, too."

She tipped her head back and looked for the butterflies, and they were very quiet, settling now back to the grass and swirling in a Disneyesque circle over the pool.

"Okay," she said, "cut it out. That's embarrassing."

The butterflies swirled upward, and for one moment, it almost seemed they formed the shape of a woman, but it was so brief, who could tell?

James bent down to kiss her, and she felt as if light burst from their joining, radiating out into the world as if to transform everything.

Love, Miranda thought, could do that.

Epilogue

Mariposa Times
May 25, 20—
The Life And Times Of Mariposans
by Rowena Reed, gossip columnist

In one of the more colorful weddings of the year,
Joshua Mad Calf, a police officer for the Mariposa Ute
Tribal Council, married Juliet Rousseau at Our Lady of
Butterflies church at 10:00 a.m. Saturday morning. The
bride wore a fitted gown of blush silk, with a sweetheart
neckline that highlighted the bride's grandmother's
pearls. Her veil was antique silk, and she carried a
bouquet of blush, red and peach rosebuds dramatically
highlighted with knots of baby-blue carnations.

   The bride's attendants were the groom's daughter, Glory Mad Calf, dressed in a princess-cut gown of soft pink lace, her hair woven with rosebuds; Dr. Desdemona Rousseau, known to locals as Dr. Desi, the vet, who wore a splendid pink and green silk sari and carried a bouquet of pink roses and green hydrangea (The draping helped disguise the doctor's broken arm!), and youngest Rousseau sister Miranda, known for her adorable little altars (the latest of which, Mariposa Running Guy, Miranda assures us will be available soon) wore a vintage Gunnysack (which this reporter remembers wearing to prom).

   The bride's parents, poet Paul Rousseau and biologist Carol Rousseau, were in prideful evidence, their faces beaming as they tossed popcorn at the bride and groom on their way out.

   The groom's family, which includes most of the Mad Calfs, the Running Moon's and the Salazars, filled the church to overflowing. The groom's mother, Helene Mad Calf, a local nurse, was resplendent in traditional buckskins.

   The reception was held at the Mariposa Hotel, where celebrities of note including skiers Max Boudrain and Christie Lundgren, along with the wan but lovely Elsa Franz, were in attendance.

   And are there more weddings in the air? The sisters were seen dancing the night away with their own lovebirds, Desi's Tamati Neville, the dashing foreigner who has brought us the delightful Black Crown; and Miranda with the elusive private detective James Marquez, who was rumored to have slipped a juicy half carat diamond on Miranda's finger.

Warm congratulations to Josh and Juliet Mad Calf and all their kin!

* * * * *

*For a sneak preview of Marie Ferrarella's
DOCTOR IN THE HOUSE,
coming to NEXT in September,
please turn the page.*

He didn't look like an unholy terror.

But maybe that reputation was exaggerated, Bailey DelMonico thought as she turned in her chair to look toward the doorway.

The man didn't seem scary at all.

Dr. Munro, or Ivan the Terrible, was tall, with an athletic build and wide shoulders. The cheekbones beneath what she estimated to be day-old stubble were prominent. His hair was light brown and just this side of unruly. Munro's hair looked as if he used his fingers for a comb and didn't care who knew it.

The eyes were brown, almost black as they were aimed at her. There was no other word for it. Aimed. As if he was debating whether or not to fire at point-blank range.

Somewhere in the back of her mind, a line from a B movie, "Be afraid—be very afraid..." whispered along the perimeter of her brain. Warning her. Almost against her will, it caused her to brace her shoulders. Bailey had to remind herself to breathe in and out like a normal person.

The chief of staff, Dr. Bennett, had tried his level best to put her at ease and had almost succeeded. But an air of tension had entered with Munro. She wondered if Dr. Bennett was bracing himself as well, bracing for some kind of disaster or explosion.

"Ah, here he is now," Harold Bennett announced needlessly. The smile on his lips was slightly forced, and the look in his gray, kindly eyes held a warning as he looked at his chief neurosurgeon. "We were just talking about you, Dr. Munro."

"Can't imagine why," Ivan replied dryly.

Harold cleared his throat, as if that would cover the less than friendly tone of voice Ivan had just displayed. "Dr. Munro, this is the young woman I was telling you about yesterday."

Now his eyes dissected her. Bailey felt as if she was undergoing a scalpel-less autopsy right then and there. "Ah yes, the Stanford Special."

He made her sound like something that was listed at the top of a third-rate diner menu. There was enough contempt in his voice to offend an entire delegation from the UN.

Summoning the bravado that her parents always claimed had been infused in her since the moment she first drew breath, Bailey put out her hand. "Hello. I'm Dr. Bailey DelMonico."

Ivan made no effort to take the hand offered to him. Instead, he slid his long, lanky form bonelessly into the chair beside her. He proceeded to move the chair ever so slightly so that there was even more space between them. Ivan faced the chief of staff, but the words he spoke were addressed to her.

"You're a doctor, DelMonico, when I say you're a doctor," he informed her coldly, sparing her only one frosty glance to punctuate the end of his statement.

Harold stifled a sigh. "Dr. Munro is going to take over your education. Dr. Munro—" he fixed Ivan with a steely gaze that had been known to send lesser doctors running for their antacids, but, as always, seemed to have no effect on the chief neurosurgeon "—I want you to award her every consideration. From now on, Dr. DelMonico is to be your shadow, your sponge and your assistant." He emphasized the last word as his eyes locked with Ivan's. "Do I make myself clear?"

For his part, Ivan seemed completely unfazed. He merely nodded, his eyes and expression unreadable. "Perfectly."

His hand was on the doorknob. Bailey sprang to her feet. Her chair made a scraping noise as she moved it back and then quickly joined the neurosurgeon before he could leave the office.

Closing the door behind him, Ivan leaned over and whispered into her ear, "Just so you know, I'm going to be your worst nightmare."

Bailey DelMonico has finally
gotten her life on track, and is
passionate about her recent career
change. Nothing will stand in the way
of her becoming a doctor...that is,
until she's paired with the sharp-tongued
Dr. Ivan Munro.

Watch the sparks fly in

Doctor in
the House

by *USA TODAY* Bestselling Author

Marie Ferrarella

Available September 2007

Intrigued? Read more at
TheNextNovel.com

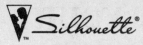

Silhouette®

Romantic
SUSPENSE

Sparked by Danger,
Fueled by Passion.

When evidence is found that Mallory Dawes
intends to sell the personal financial information
of government employees to "the Russian,"
OMEGA engages undercover agent Cutter Smith.
Tailing her all the way to France, Cutter is
fighting a growing attraction to Mallory while at
the same time having to determine her connection
to "the Russian." Is Mallory really the mouse in
this game of cat and mouse?

Look for

Stranded with a Spy

by *USA TODAY* bestselling author

Merline Lovelace

October 2007.

Also available October wherever you buy books:

BULLETPROOF MARRIAGE *(Mission: Impassioned)*
by Karen Whiddon

A HERO'S REDEMPTION *(Haven)* by Suzanne McMinn

TOUCHED BY FIRE by Elizabeth Sinclair

REQUEST YOUR FREE BOOKS!

2 FREE NOVELS PLUS 2 FREE GIFTS!

Silhouette® Romantic

SUSPENSE

Sparked by Danger, Fueled by Passion!

YES! Please send me 2 FREE Silhouette® Romantic Suspense novels and my 2 FREE gifts. After receiving them, if I don't wish to receive any more books, I can return the shipping statement marked "cancel." If I don't cancel, I will receive 4 brand-new novels every month and be billed just $4.24 per book in the U.S., or $4.99 per book in Canada, plus 25¢ shipping and handling per book plus applicable taxes, if any*. That's a savings of at least 15% off the cover price! I understand that accepting the 2 free books and gifts places me under no obligation to buy anything. I can always return a shipment and cancel at any time. Even if I never buy another book from Silhouette, the two free books and gifts are mine to keep forever.

240 SDN EEX6 340 SDN EEYJ

Name	(PLEASE PRINT)	
Address		Apt. #
City	State/Prov.	Zip/Postal Code

Signature (if under 18, a parent or guardian must sign)

Mail to the Silhouette Reader Service™:
IN U.S.A.: P.O. Box 1867, Buffalo, NY 14240-1867
IN CANADA: P.O. Box 609, Fort Erie, Ontario L2A 5X3

Not valid to current Silhouette Intimate Moments subscribers.

Want to try two free books from another line?
Call 1-800-873-8635 or visit www.morefreebooks.com.

* Terms and prices subject to change without notice. NY residents add applicable sales tax. Canadian residents will be charged applicable provincial taxes and GST. This offer is limited to one order per household. All orders subject to approval. Credit or debit balances in a customer's account(s) may be offset by any other outstanding balance owed by or to the customer. Please allow 4 to 6 weeks for delivery.

Your Privacy: Silhouette is committed to protecting your privacy. Our Privacy Policy is available online at www.eHarlequin.com or upon request from the Reader Service. From time to time we make our lists of customers available to reputable firms who may have a product or service of interest to you. If you would prefer we not share your name and address, please check here. ☐

SRS07

Silhouette Desire

There was only one man for the job—
an impossible-to-resist maverick
she knew she didn't dare fall for.

MAVERICK
(#1827)

BY *NEW YORK TIMES*
BESTSELLING AUTHOR
JOAN HOHL

"Will You Do It for One Million Dollars?"

Any other time, Tanner Wolfe would have balked at being
hired by a woman. Yet Brianna Stewart was desperate to
engage the infamous bounty hunter. The price was just
high enough to gain Tanner's interest...Brianna's beauty
definitely strong enough to keep it. But he wasn't about
to allow her to tag along on his mission. He worked
alone. Always had. Always would. However, he'd never
confronted a more determined client than Brianna. She
wasn't taking no for an answer—not about anything.

Perhaps a million-dollar bounty was not the only thing
this maverick was about to gain....

Look for MAVERICK

Available October 2007 wherever you buy books.

Ria Sterling has the gift—or is it a curse?—
of seeing a person's future in his or her
photograph. Unfortunately, when detective
Carrick Jones brings her a missing person's
case, she glimpses his partner's ID—and
sees imminent murder. And when her vision
comes true, Ria becomes the prime suspect.
Carrick isn't convinced this beautiful woman
committed the crime...but does he believe
she has the special powers to solve it?

Look for

Seeing Is Believing

by

Kate Austin

Available October
wherever you buy books.

Silhouette®

Romantic
SUSPENSE

COMING NEXT MONTH

SRSCNM0907